THE RESIDENTS OF ALABASTER COURT

NITA CLARKE

Published in the United States of America

ISBN 978-1-970703-18-4 (Paperback)
ISBN 978-1-970703-19-1 (Hardback)
ISBN 978-1-970703-20-7 (Ebook)

For Book Rights Adaption and other Rights Permission.

Call us at toll-free **601-914-6178.**

DEDICATION

To my muse!

CONTENTS

BOOK VII: THE BLACKWELL'S

BOOK VIII: THE RESIDENTS OF ALABASTER COURT

BOOK I
Charlotte Davis

- CHAPTER 1 -

MEET CARL SPENSER

The sound of screeching tires resonated throughout the wet streets of the city of Lexington, Kentucky as the police cruiser flashed its lights and pierced the air with its siren. Veteran Officer Thomas Patterson and his rookie partner, Officer Carl Spenser, were headed toward the suburban area of the city to answer the call that had just come across the police dispatch. The rain was falling steadily and glistened in the early morning air. It was 0315 the morning of Saturday, August 16, 2003.

"Well," stated Patterson as he sped down Highway 75 toward Alabaster Court, "looks like you're gonna get your initiation with this one."

The young man sitting in the passenger seat of the cruiser inhaled deeply.

"Bet you've seen a lot of dead bodies in your career."

"Too many," Patterson answered as he kept a steady stare on the road. "Thought I'd gotten away from all of this when I left Chicago."

From a short distance the sound of other sirens filled the air as first responder vehicles headed down Alabaster Drive that emptied into the Court; a firetruck, ambulance, crime scene unit and, the Coroner. So many lights were flashing brightly in the dark that it appeared to be the dawning of the sun coming up to kiss the earth.

The young officer swallowed as he opened the cruiser door, now parked in front of 11729 Alabaster Court.

"Got your note pad?" Patterson asked.

"Yeah," Spenser answered sarcastically, "fully prepared."

The front door to the house was opened and the other residents of the Court were now beginning to come outside of their homes to stand on their porches, or staring out of a bedroom window. Officer Patterson opened the front door and was met by the grieving father, fifty-one-year-old Joe Davis, in his robe and pajamas. His wife, forty-nine-year-old Pat Davis was sitting on the couch in the living room sobbing and stroking a large calico cat.

"Mr. Davis, I'm Officer Patterson and this is my partner Officer Spenser. We're so sorry for your loss."

It was apparent that the man was fighting back tears, tears that had obviously been flowing just prior to him opening the door. Without saying a word, he led the two police officers outside to the back of the house where the young woman lay face down in the pool. She was fully clothed in jeans and a shirt, one of her red Converse tennis shoes was missing, her long blond hair flowing with the movement of the water in the pool. Blood was oozing out of her head and spilling into the pool. The young Officer stood frozen by the side of the pool, staring at the scene.

"Spence," Patterson called out, catching him off guard. "Why don't you go inside with the Davises and get as much information from the parents as you can. I'll stay out here with the Crime Scene Investigators." Seconds later, the scene was filled with the people that had now come to do their jobs.

The interview was difficult for both the young officer and, the mother and father.

"I know this is very hard for you but can you tell me what happened?"

"Charlotte was our only child," Mrs. Davis said as she continued to stroke the calico cat. "She was only 22-years-old. She was a student at the University of Florida in Jacksonville studying to be a nurse. She was home for the summer." The mother began to cry again. Her husband leaned forward to cover her with his arm.

Officer Spenser wrote the information down on his note pad as the conversation continued.

"Who found the body?" he asked.

"I did," said Mr. Davis. "I heard a noise that woke me up so I got out of bed and went downstairs thinking the cat had knocked something over. When I got to the kitchen, I noticed through the window that the pool lights were still on. I went outside to the deck to turn the lights off…and that's when I saw her, floating on top of the water." His voice quivered and he began to sob.

The Officer paused momentarily so that the parents could catch their breath.

"I noticed your daughter had on street clothes," said the young officer. "Had she been out the night before?"

"Yes," Mr. Davis stated. "She and her boyfriend, Brad Simmons, and some of their friends had gone out for the evening. My wife and I went to bed about 10:30pm, after the nightly news. Charlotte wasn't home yet."

"I'll need Brad's phone number, and I'll need the names of her friends and any information you can give me about them."

"Of course," said Mr. Davis.

A picture on the mantle of a young woman in cap and gown caught the attention of the young officer. He walked over to the picture and lifted it from the mantle.

"Is this Charlotte?" He asked.

"Yes," replied Mr. Davis with a tremble in his voice. "That's our Charlotte."

"One more thing," the young officer said. "Can you think of anyone that might want to hurt your daughter? An ex-boyfriend? A jealous friend?"

"Of course not," Mrs. Davis said quickly, sitting straight up. "Charlotte was a good girl, everybody loved her. She wanted to help people that were hurting, that's why she wanted to be a nurse."

The conversation between the Davises and Officer Spenser was interrupted by Betty Eliason, a resident of the court and close friend of Pat Davis, who came into the house with arms opened wide.

"Oh Pat! What happened?" Betty Eliason asked with tears in her eyes.

"It's Charlotte," Pat answered, standing to hug her. "She's gone!"

"What do you mean 'she's gone'?" Betty asked.

"She's dead, Betty." Pat said. "Just like that, our daughter is dead."

"Ma'am," Officer Spenser said, speaking to the woman who had walked in. "May I ask who you are?"

"I'm Betty Eliason." The woman answered. "I'm Pat's friend. I need to be here with her."

The two walked together to the kitchen while Joe Davis continued to talk with Officer Spenser. Within just a few moments, Homicide Detective Matt Parker joined Officer Spenser in the living room of the Davis home.

"This is the information I've gathered so far." Officer Spenser said to the Detective, handing him the page from the notebook. "Officer Patterson is out back with Crime Scene."

"Thanks." Detective Parker said as he took over the investigation.

Officer Spenser found his way to the back of the house and outside to the pool. Again, he found himself staring, this time at the empty pool. By this time the crime scene had been marked and cleared, and the body had been removed.

"Looks like the body was only in the pool for a short period of time." The investigator said. "Cause of death, for now before an autopsy is blunt force trauma to the head. There are also marks around her neck as though the perpetrator tried to strangle her and then pushed her body into the pool. I'll know more when I get her on the table."

The Court was quiet and the sun was beginning to rise when the two police officers drove away from Alabaster Court. Many of the residents were now standing on their lawns as first responder vehicles made their way back down Alabaster Drive. Both Officer Patterson and Officer Spenser were quiet as they made their way back to the Police Station to make their report.

The night may have ended but for Officer Spenser, the scene would haunt him for what seemed like a lifetime.

CHAPTER 2

MISSING

Forty-one-year-old Detective Carl Spenser slammed his hand down on the snooze button on the alarm clock next to his bed and rolled over for just fifteen more precious minutes of sleep. When the alarm clock sounded for a second time, he crawled out of bed, turned the tv to the news, hopped on his treadmill for a twenty-minute run and headed for a ten-minute shower with tepid water. The aroma of coffee brewing in the kitchen began to fill the apartment. After getting dressed he savored a cup of hot black coffee with two slices of toast with strawberry jam. It was the same routine every day; nothing ever seemed to change, except the date…it was Monday, April 27, 2020.

The short drive to the police station from his apartment only took fifteen minutes each day. Arriving a few minutes before 0800, he made his way to his desk and continued his early morning routine; a second cup of black coffee and a doughnut that someone had bought and left in the lounge. Within a few more minutes his partner Detective Sheila Michaels arrived. The two had only been partners for the past three years, ever since she was promoted to Detective. In that short period of time, however, they had established a great working rapport and a strong friendship.

"Morning Spence." Sheila said, sitting down at her desk that faced her partner's.

"Hey." Carl answered. "How was your weekend?"

"Pretty good." Sheila said. "Ed and I took the kids to the Louisville Zoo. It was nice. How about you?"

"Oh, Same old same old," Carl answered. "Little tv, a few beers. Nothing much."

"I'm serious, you need to get a life!" Sheila whispered.

"I have a life." Carl answered. "Freedom to do my thing."

The conversation ended abruptly when the phone began to ring.

"Missing Persons, Detective Spenser." Carl said as he answered the phone.

"Good morning," said Detective Donovan, Head of Missing Persons. "We have a missing eighteen-year-old girl." The voice on the other end of the phone stated. "Been missing since Friday evening. Parents called 911 after they found her bed empty Saturday morning. Name's Marie Jackson. Address is 11729 Alabaster Court."

Carl's face suddenly took on a look of shock.

"Did you say 11729 Alabaster Court?"

"Yes," the voice on the other end of the phone said, "I've got the full incident report filed by an Officer Bob Carver here in my office. You can pick it up on your way out."

Carl hung up the phone and stared into space.

"Carl?" Sheila said. "Are you okay?"

"I don't know," Carl answered. "We have a missing eighteen-year-old girl. Her address is 11729 Alabaster Court. My first case as a Patrol Officer was at that very same address; murder of a twenty-two-year-old woman. The case went cold almost immediately. I'll never forget it. She was floating face down in the backyard pool."

"Oh no!" Sheila responded. "Do you think it's the same family?"

"I don't think so. She was an only child at the time." Carl said.

After a few moments of silence, Carl announced to Sheila that it was time to head out to investigate the case. The two stopped by Detective Donovan's office to pick up the police report. Sheila could tell that Carl was pretty shaken by the case.

"You gonna' be okay?" She asked.

"Yeah, sure…sure." He answered. "Just took me back to that night, seventeen years ago. I was just a rookie cop partnered with a veteran cop. Patterson was his name. He had transferred from Chicago after seeing too much of what we saw that night."

Carl continued as the two walked toward the car. "She was just 22! Home for summer break from the University in Florida. Forensics showed that it was blunt force trauma to the head with a foreign object that was never found. She had been choked to almost dead and then thrown in the family pool where she apparently drowned. She put up a good fight though; there were defense markings on her hands and arms. Her parents were just devastated as you can imagine. As I said, the case went cold really quickly. The only thing similar to evidence was her missing red Converse tennis shoe. There was no blood, no footprints, no fingerprints. Every once-in-a while I still check with homicide to see if anything's come up about the case."

Once inside the car Carl resumed his story. "Her name was Charlotte Davis I will never forget her or her parents. I've seen things in my years as a Police Officer since then but nothing made me want to lose it like that case."

As the two neared the Court, Carl began to feel the exact same feelings that he had felt some seventeen years before at this very same place. He took a deep breath and pulled into the Court in front of 11729. Everything looked pretty much the same, a little older and the house had been painted an entirely different color. As Carl and Sheila neared the house, Carl began to breathe heavily. Suddenly, the door opened and a man was standing in the doorway. For a moment, Carl saw Mr. Davis and froze in his tracks. Sheila quickly took the lead.

"Mr Jackson?" the man nodded his head yes. "I'm Detective Michaels and this is my partner Detective Spenser."

Carl lowered his head and raised it to come eye-to-eye with the man in the doorway."

"Mr. Jackson, we're here to investigate your missing person's report that came through the 911 system on Saturday." Carl said. "May we come in?"

"What took you so long?" The man asked angrily. "My daughter called 911 on Saturday and nobody came. What happened to the Amber Alert? And my name is Dupuis, not Jackson!"

"I'm sorry, Mr. Dupuis. I didn't know."

"Sir, a missing persons' case requires us to wait 48 hours. That would be today." Carl continued. "And your daughter is eighteen; Amber Alerts are only for children up to seventeen-years-old."

"His granddaughter." Ms. Jackson said, inviting the two Detectives inside the house. "Please, have a seat." Ms. Jackson said. "Would you like something to drink?"

"No, thank you." Carl answered.

"Someone did come here on Saturday, dad, don't you remember?" Ms. Jackson said. "A very nice policeman came and took the report. He also told us that it would be 48 hours."

"We'd like to ask a few questions, if you don't mind." Carl said. "Did your daughter go out of the house Friday?"

"Yes." Ms. Jackson answered. "She went to her girlfriend's house, or at least we thought that's where she was. I called the girl, Nikki is her name, and she said that Marie had not been there at all." She began to sob.

"We'll need Marie's friend's full name and phone number, address." Carl continued. "In fact, it would be helpful if you have any information about any of the other friends that Marie might have. Someone might have information that could help us find your daughter."

"Of course." Ms. Jackson said. "Marie keeps all her information in her laptop in her room. Let me get it for you." After a few moments Ms. Jackson returned with the laptop.

"Do you mind if we take this with us?" Steve said. "I'll be sure to get it back to you."

"Ok." Ms. Jackson said. "Anything I can do to help."

"Do you remember what Marie was wearing the last time you saw her?" Carl asked.

After a few moments of thinking, Ms. Jackson described Marie as wearing a pair of jeans and a blue shirt. "She had on running shoes, her blue ones, I think. I'm really not sure about the color of her shoes. She also had her jean jacket with her; I told her to bring it with her because it was a little chilly outside. The last time I saw her she was getting into her car."

"What kind of a car does she have?" Carl asked.

"A 2014 Subaru Forester. It's olive green."

"Nice car." Sheila answered. "Graduation gift?"

"Sort of." Ms. Jackson said. "We got it for her last year as a pre-graduation gift. She needed a nice, dependable car to drive to her college and back on weekends.

"Have you tried calling Marie on her cell phone?" Carl asked.

"Only about one-hundred times." She answered.

"Can you tell us what kinds of things Marie and her friends did for recreation?" Carl asked.

"I know she enjoyed going to the Mall with her friends." Ms. Jackson said. "But this is her senior year so she has been really busy preparing to graduate so there's been a lot of 'getting ready' for college going on." Ms. Jackson continued. "Where will Marie be attending college?" Sheila asked.

"Eastern Kentucky University, she wants to be an English teacher so she'll be studying Education." Ms. Jackson smiled with pride as she described her daughter's plans for the future.

"That sounds wonderful." Sheila said. "Sounds like a very intelligent young lady."

"Very much so." Ms. Jackson said. "She's actually the first one of our family to go to college. I went to a two-year program to become a Secretary, or Administrative Assistant as they call it now. Her father went to College down south. So, we're very proud of Marie's accomplishments."

"Is her father in Lexington?" Carl asked.

"He was, but we're divorced now. He's back down south but Marie and he spend time together during the summer and spring break. He also comes here during the holidays for a few days."

"What is his name?"

"Drew Jackson."

"We'll need his address and phone number as well." Carl said.

"Sure." She writes her ex-husband's name, address and phone number down on a piece of paper and gives it to Carl."

"Is there a chance that Marie is with her father?"

"I called him when I first discovered her missing but he swore she was not there." Ms. Jackson said, raising her voice slightly. "He actually told me to call the police. I don't know if I should believe him or not."

"Don't worry about that, Ms. Jackson." Carl said. "We'll check him out." Can you think of anyone that might want to hurt Marie? A boyfriend? A jealous friend?"

"No, actually." Ms. Jackson said. "She really doesn't have a boyfriend, just a few girls and guys that hang out together. When they're not busy they usually go roller skating or they all come over her to swim. I just have no idea what has happened to her."

"We are definitely going to follow all of the leads you've given us and I can assure we'll do everything we can to find your daughter." Carl said, putting his hand on Ms. Jackson's shoulder."

Ms. Jackson's eyes began to fill with tears.

"I'm going to trust you finding her!" She said.

"You can trust that we will do our best." Carl answered. "And I promise we'll be in touch with anything we find out."

"Thank you," Ms. Jackson said as she followed the Detectives toward the front door. Once inside the car, Sheila asked Carl if he had any ideas at all as to where Marie Jackson could be.

"To be very honest with you, "Carl said. "I have no idea. I've been in Missing Persons now for eight years and I truly have no clue. But we made the promise that we would find her daughter so let's get to it."

"Where do we start?" Sheila asked.

"With the father, of course. So many missing persons have been taken by family so we'll start with Drew Jackson."

As they drove away, Cora Jackson was still standing at the door watching as the car sped away from Alabaster Court.

- CHAPTER 3 -

FOUND

It had been several months since Carl had checked in with Homicide Cold Case regarding Charlotte Davis' case. Marie Jackson's missing persons' case had sparked a sudden desire to look into any progress that might have been made on the Davis case. The new Detective in charge of Homicide Cold Case was Steve Martinez. Carl had not yet met Martinez but was anxious to meet him and find out anything he had come across in the form of evidence on the Charlotte Davis case.

Steve Martinez had joined the force around the year 2000; became a police officer after two years in Law School, and became a Homicide Detective six years later. For approximately ten-years, Martinez served the Homicide Department and had now transferred to Homicide Cold Case. Carl had done his homework, looking into Martinez's record. He learned that he was married to Monica Hernandez Martinez. The couple had one son and two daughters. Born and raised in Albuquerque, New Mexico, Martinez ended up in Lexington like so many young people do…the University of Kentucky.

Back in the office again, Carl settled in to read his phone messages and catch up on the missing persons' cases.

"Any news on the Marie Jackson case yet?" Carl asked Sheila.

"Yes, as a matter of fact. I called Drew Jackson, Marie's father. He swore he had no idea where his daughter was." Sheila said. "He asked me to make sure we called him back with any information we find. Actually, he sounded pretty convincing to me."

"Hum." Carl said. "I didn't think she was there, especially with her car still parked at her house."

"Well, I also spoke to several of her friends who said there was a big party that Friday night down by the River. Senior celebration." Sheila said. "Only one of her friends actually admitted to seeing her there…a young man by the name of Jaron Franklin."

"And he was the only one that fest up, huh?" Carl asked.

"Yep. I think he was scared out of his skin that he was going to be in big trouble since the party wasn't supposed to be happening. He talked as though there was a lot of liquor and weed." Sheila said.

"Were you able to contact the girl Marie was supposed to be spending the night with? Betcha' she knows something."

"I got ahold of her mother." Sheila continued. "Nikki wasn't home from school yet. Maybe we can make some visits this afternoon,"

"You got it! Any progress on the Charlotte Davis case yet?" Sheila asked, sipping her cup of coffee. "I know that's where you were. Any time you're late to the office or don't let me know that's you'll be late I know you're checking on information about that case."

"Well, yeah, that's where I was." Carl answered. "Nothing yet. Homicide Cold Case does have a new Head…a Detective Steve Martinez. Hopefully I'll get the opportunity to meet him sometime soon." Carl continued as he leafed through the messages. "Well, isn't that strange! Here's a message from Martinez asking me to return his call!"

Carl grabbed his phone and dialed Martinez's extension.

"Homicide Cold Case, Griffin speaking." The voice on the other end of the phone said. "May I help you?"

"Yes." Carl said. "This is Detective Carl Spenser with Missing Persons, returning Detective Martinez's call. Is he available?"

"Hold please."

"Thank you."

Moments went by and finally the phone was answered.

"Detective Martinez."

"Hello." Carl answered. "This is Detective Carl Spenser, returning your call."

"Hello, Detective Spenser." Martinez said. "Thank you for getting back to me so fast. I've been going through the Homicide Cold Cases and ran across one that had your name on it as one of the Officers that was first responder that night. You were partnered with an Officer Patterson who has since retired. The victim's name is Charlotte Davis. Do you remember the case?"

"Do I!!" Carl answered. "I've been haunted by that case for seventeen-years now. I check in every one in a while to see if there's any leads but all these years not a single thing has changed."

"To be honest with you," Martinez said. "that's what got my attention. Not a single piece of evidence was found, just the dead body with a missing red Converse tennis shoe."

"That's right." Carl said. "The autopsy showed that she was barely alive, but alive, when she was thrown or pushed into the pool. She drowned to death, after being beat up and choked nearly to death."

"Yes, I saw that in the report. Why don't we get together and talk sometime soon?" Martinez said.

"That'd be great." Carl answered. "I've got a case right now that needs my full attention, but I have a feeling that it's going to be ending soon so let's just say…Monday?"

"Monday sounds great." Martinez said. "Meet me for lunch? Say 1:00 o'clock?"

"J Alexander's?" Carl suggested. "At the Summit?"

"Perfect." Martinez said. "Until then."

"Goodbye."

Carl sat back in his chair and put his hands behind his head. "Martinez wants to meet with me on Monday."

"I heard…J Alexander's for lunch." Sheila responded.

"Yeah, well, we've got that long to find out where Marie Jackson is. Let's take a ride to the river." Carl said as he gathered his belongings together. "Do we know exactly where this party was?"

"Well, Jaron Franklin said it was by the picnic areas." Sheila said. "I'm sure it won't be too hard to find if that much activity was going on."

"I'll drive." Carl said. The two made their way to the garage and once in the car, headed toward the river. The morning was warm with a gentle breeze and the sun was hidden by the darkness of the clouds. The drive itself took a good thirty minutes and the two began to look for a driveway as soon as they crossed the bridge.

"How do you know there's a road here?" Sheila asked.

"There's always a dirt road somewhere off this bridge."

Carl veered off to the right of the bridge and down a rough gravel road that led to the picnic areas.

"Is this a legal road?" Sheila asked as the two bounced up and down in the car, hitting every hole in the road.

"I doubt it, but it looks like someone's been using it enough to make a road out of it." Carl answered. "I hope it doesn't lead us into the river!"

The drive on the dusty road lasted approximately another fifteen minutes until the road stopped abruptly at a grassy plain that lead to the paved, main road.

"Left, or right?" Carl said.

"Left." Sheila answered laughing. "I'm a south paw."

After another long drive, Carl finally pulled the car up to the picnic areas along the banks of the river. The road curved around the bend, exposing several picnic sites with bar-be-que pits, picnic tables and trash cans. Every site looked neat and clean as Carl and Sheila slowly continued their exploration. Finally, small amounts of trash began to appear along the road.

"Looks like we're getting close to something." Carl said as he pulled the car over.

Carl and Sheila jumped out of the car and began to walk along the bank of the river, eventually meeting up with what appeared to be the place where the party was being held. There were beer cans, wine bottles, paper plates and napkins, and food strewn all around the full trash can. There were also balloons that had been popped and laying on the ground, obviously a way to acknowledge the location of the party.

"What a mess!" Sheila said.

"Reminds me of some of the parties I sneaked out to when I was young." Carl added.

The two Detectives began to dig through the debris of the party, looking to find any king of evidence that Marie Jackson had been there. Several feet down the river, Sheila yelled out that she had found a cell phone underneath one of the picnic tables. Carl ran to meet her.

"She probably came to the party with someone who brought her to wherever she is now. My guess is that someone picked her up at the girl's house, where she was supposed to be spending the night…Nikki. Someone else picked her up from Nikki's house and brought her here. Do me a favor, Sheila. Check the phone to see if there's a 'mom' or 'mother', some name these kids might call their mothers these days."

"Good call." Sheila said. "There's a 'momma'."

"Give her a call." Carl said as he impatiently waited for someone to answer.

"Hello." A woman's voice said. "Is that you, Marie? Where are you?"

"Hello." Sheila responded. "This is Detective Michaels from Missing Persons. And who is this?"

"This is Cora Jackson." The woman said. "Detective Michaels, did you find Marie?"

"It's Cora Jackson." Sheila whispered.

Carl took the phone from Sheila.

"Ms. Jackson, this is Detective Spenser."

"Oh no!" She said anxiously. "Did something happen to Marie? How did you get her phone??"

"No, we have no proof that anything's happened to Marie." Carl said, trying to calm her down. "In fact, we found her phone at the picnic grounds by the river. Looks like a bunch of kids had a party…"

"I told her she couldn't go to that party because I knew there would be a lot of drinking and God only knows what else!" Cora said angrily. "She asked me about it a couple weeks ago. We had a big argument about it. She said she was old enough to make her own decisions and I told her as long as she lived under my roof, she would follow my rules."

"So, she probably got someone to pick her up at Nikki's house and bring her to the party." Carl said. "We found her phone under a picnic table. I don't think she's in any harm; probably at a friend's house, and since you two had an argument, she's probably just hiding out."

"Oh, my goodness! You don't think she's run away from home, do you?"

"No. I don't believe so, Ms. Jackson." Carl answered. "Like I said, she's probably just hiding out with friends. What we need to do is get the message out to all of her friends that you want her to come home regardless of what happened. And I think we need to start with Nikki!"

"I have Nikki's mother's phone number." Ms. Jackson said. "I talked to her on Saturday. She's the one that told me that Marie had not spent the night there. Nikki wasn't at home at the time."

"Do you have the address?" Carl asked.

"Yes." Cora answered. Sheila quickly wrote down the address and gave it to Carl. "Her name is Alice Donovan."

"We'll be in touch as soon as we find out anything."

The rain had begun to fall ever so slightly when Carl and Sheila drove up to the Donovan house. Carl knocked on the door and a woman answered, more than likely it was Alice Donovan.

"Hello ma'am." Carl said. "I'm Detective Spenser and this is my partner Detective Michaels from Missing Persons. May we come in?"

The woman seemed flustered by the announcement but opened the door wide enough for the two Detectives to enter the house.

"What can I do for you, Detectives?" Alice asked, inviting them to sit at the kitchen table. "Did something happen?"

"We're investigating a Missing Persons' case…Marie Jackson…"

"Oh, yes." Alice said. "Her mother called me looking for Marie. Something about her being here, spending the night with my daughter, Nikki. She wasn't here."

"Well, we have reason to believe that your daughter might have information that could lead us to Marie's location." Carl said. "Is she at home now?"

"Yes, she's in her bedroom." Alice said cautiously, calling out to her daughter. "Nikki, come here, please!"

The young girl came into the kitchen. "Yes, momma."

"These two Detectives are here to talk to you about Marie Jackson. Do you know anything about where she might be?"

The young girl was quiet and lowered her head.

"Nikki!" Alice said. "Do you know something about her whereabouts? This is very serious! When I told you that Mrs. Jackson called, you said you had no idea about where Marie could be…were you lying to me?"

"I'm sorry, momma." Nikki said, beginning to cry. "She begged me not to say anything."

"Say anything about what?" Carl asked. "Do you have any idea where Marie could be now?"

"No, sir." Nikki said, beginning to cry. "All I know is that two friends of hers from the University picked her up Friday night on the street corner by her house. She asked me not to say anything to anyone, just that she was spending the night with me. I'm so sorry."

"These two friends…do you have any idea where they live?" Carl asked. "No, sir." Nikki said. "All I know is that they live in one of the apartments on campus."

"So…do you know any of your friends that might have that information?" Carl asked.

"The only one of our friends that I know might know who they are would be Jaron." Nikki said. "I have his number."

"Jaron Franklin?? Oh! I already have Jaron's number!" Sheila said.

"Well, we thank you for your time, Mrs. Donovan." Carl said. "And thank you, Nikki. I'm sure you've learned a very valuable lesson here…"

"Yes, sir." Nikki answered. "I won't let any of my friends put me in that situation ever again."

Carl and Sheila got back in the car and headed to the Franklin house. It did not take much encouragement to get Jaron to talk about the party, the two friends that had picked Marie up and exactly where they lived.

"I'm sure there's going to be some very heavy conversation going on today with these parents and kids!" Sheila said, as Carl drove the car toward the University. The apartment was on the second floor. Carl and Sheila climbed the stairs and knocked on the door.

"Who is it?" Said the voice on the other side of the door.

"Detectives Spenser and Michaels. Please open the door".

The muffled sound of voices and people moving around in the apartment could be heard. The door opened and a young woman appeared.

"Can I help you?" She said.

"Can we come in?" Carl said. "We are following up on a missing persons' case…we know she's here."

The young woman opened the door for the two Detectives to enter into the apartment.

"Look, Detective." She said. I don't want any trouble. Yes, she's here.

Marie!" The young woman yelled out. "You need to come out here now. Marie?"

The bedroom door opened slowly and a young woman appeared in the doorway. She was wearing the exact clothes that Cora Jackson described; jeans, a blue shirt and tennis shoes.

"Are you Marie Jackson?" Carl asked.

"Yes, sir." She whispered.

"Get your things, you're going home." Carl said softly. "Your mother has been very worried about you and all she wants is for you to come home, so let's put her heart at ease." Marie put her head down and began to cry.

"Come on," Sheila said, putting her arm around Marie's shoulder. "Let's get you home."

Marie and the Detectives walked toward the car.

"My mom called you?" Marie asked, once inside of the car.

"Yes, she did." Carl said. "That's how worried she was, so she called us to find you and we're so happy to find you safe. Do you know how many young people are never found or are found in terrible situations…or even dead? Never to see their parents again?"

"Yes, sir." Marie answered. "I'm sorry. I really wanted to go to that party and she didn't want me to go. I'm eighteen, about to go to college. I didn't see any harm in me going."

"Well, your mother did think you could be harmed. Something could have happened to you and you could have never been found…especially down at the river."

The car drove down Alabaster Drive and onto the Court. Carl pulled into the Jackson house driveway and got out of the car. Sheila opened the back door and helped Marie out of the car. As the three of them began to walk toward the house, Cora Jackson came to the door. She ran from the house to the driveway where Marie was standing.

"Marie!" Cora yelled out. "Thank God, you're home and safe!" Cora wrapped her arms around her daughter and Marie returned the hug.

"I'm sorry, momma." Marie said sadly. "I'm really sorry!"

The two continued to hug as they walked up to the door.

"Thank you, Detectives." Cora Jackson said as she looked back.

Carl and Sheila smiled and waved as they got back into the car.

"You know, Carl," Sheila said. "all of this could have been avoided if the two of them would have only talked instead of arguing."

"That's true, Sheila." Carl answered as he turned out of the court and onto Alabaster Drive. "I wish all of our cases would wind up this easy and positive."

CHAPTER 4

11741 ALABASTER COURT

Detective Martinez waved his hand and stood up so that Detective Spenser could see where he was sitting. Carl saw him and headed over to the table at J Alexander's in the Summit.

"Looks pretty busy here today." Carl said shaking Steve's hand. "Nice to meet you."

"You, too, brother." Steve responded. The two sat down at the table.

"Now how did you know it was me?" Carl asked.

"'Cause you looked like you were looking for a missing person!" Steve said laughing. Nah, just kidding. I looked you up in the staff directory, just like you probably did me."

Just then the waiter appeared and asked what the two would like to drink. "Sweet Tea," Carl said.

"Typical Kentuckian!" Steve said. "I'll have coffee, black, please."

"That's right! You're from Albuquerque." Carl teased. The two laughed. "So, did you find your missing person like you were hoping?" Steve asked.

"Yeah. We did." Carl answered. "The kind of case I like; no one hurt, no victim, everybody alive.

"Far cry from Homicide!" Steve said. "There's always a suspect, and a dead body. Which brings me to Charlotte Davis. What a case that is; no evidence but a missing shoe and an autopsy report."

"I know." Carl responded. "This case has bugged me for seventeen years now. I bet I've been to Homicide Cold Case a dozen times over the years and nothing's changed. Strange thing though…the young girl that was missing? Lives in the house where Charlotte Davis died."

"You're kidding." Steve said, surprised. "That is strange."

"No, I'm serious." Carl said. "I had to go back there for an entirely different case; same house."

"Wow! Well, I was looking through the Davis case file when I saw your name, yours and your former partner. I figured you might be able to give me some insight on the case." Steve said. "I plan to re-open the case and I was hoping you might want to work with me, try to put an end to this cold case."

"Would I!" Carl said excited. "We'll have to go through the chain of command to get permission…"

"I'm way ahead of you." Steve said. "I've already put in the papers to 'borrow' you for as long as it takes. What I want to do is interview everyone that lives in Alabaster Court; get their stories, what they've heard, what they've seen…"

"There's a Home Owners Association that we can get the names of the residents of each house." Carl replied. "I'll work on that."

"And I'll work on a schedule so you can spend most of your time in Missing Persons and the rest with Homicide. You'll truly be a Spenser for Hire!" Steve joked.

"Ah, just so you know? You're not the first lawman that pulled that on me." Carl said. "but it's Spenser with a 'c' not an 's'!"

Betty Eliason, whose family was originally from Ohio, and her divorced daughter, forty-four-year-old Meghan, resided at 11741 Alabaster Court, in the house located on the right corner of Alabaster Drive and the Court at the time of the murder of Charlotte Davis. Betty had come across the street on that night to console her friend, Pat. Betty and Pat Davis had become close friends almost from the very first time they met. Pat brought over a bottle of wine and a box of chocolates to welcome the Eliason's to Alabaster Court and after several hours of friendly conversation, the two became inseparable.

Betty and her husband, Henry, had moved to Lexington from Ohio to be near their children in the year 2000 after he retired from the Army. Unfortunately, Henry would have a heart attack just two short years after he and Betty bought the house. The year before, their youngest child Meghan, moved out of her apartment that was just on the outside of the Court, to share the house with her parents.

Meghan had been a student at the University of Kentucky and after graduating with her Degree in Information Technology made the decision to live and work in Lexington, accepting a job as an IT specialist at a local bank. She and Charlotte had become great friends as well, during that short time before her death, spending time shopping together, going out with friends and talking about the men in their lives. Meghan had been married for approximately five years before she discovered that her husband was having an affair. She chose quickly to divorce him and moved out of her apartment. Her husband, Max Douglas, remained in the apartment.

Betty's middle child, forty-seven-year-old Grace and her husband Adam Peterson also lived in Lexington, Adam's home. Grace met her husband-to-be at a Derby party and began dating shortly thereafter. The two would marry two-years later when Adam graduated with his Master's in Business Administration and accepted a job with the local Government. Grace opened a small seamstress shop in the spare room in their home where she made curtains; sewed dresses, pants, blouses, shirts, pillows and other items for her customers while caring for their three children.

Daniel, Betty's oldest child, followed in his father's footsteps by joining the Army after completing college at home in Ohio. After finishing Dental School, Daniel spent several tours of duty overseas before being shipped out to Afghanistan in 2003. It would be in Afghanistan that Daniel would meet his future bride, a Reservist named Jennifer Parker who served as a Dental Hygienist. Daniel and Jennifer began to date, finally married and lived on several Army Bases around the country. The two had one child, Daniel, Jr. Daniel retired as a Major at Fort Knox, Kentucky after twenty-years of service to the Army and opened a Dental Clinic in Louisville. Jennifer retired from the Reserves and joined her husband as his Dental Assistant

It was a beautiful spring day when Carl and Homicide Detective Cold Case Steve Martinez made their way back to Alabaster Court to investigate the cold case death of Charlotte Davis. Carl drove the car to the driveway of Betty Eliason's house. He had chosen to interview her first since he remembered her from the night of Charlotte Davis' murder.

Meghan Eliason Douglas answered the front door. Carl smiled and showed his badge to her.

"Hello." He said. "I'm Detective Carl Spenser and this is my partner, Detective Steve Martinez. We're here to speak with Betty Eliason. Is she here?"

"Yes." Meghan answered curiously. "I'm her daughter, Meghan. Please, come in. She's in the kitchen."

Carl and Steve followed Meghan where they found Betty sitting at the kitchen table drinking a cup of coffee and reading the newspaper. Carl recognized Betty from 2003 when she had entered the Davis' home to comfort Pat Davis. She was a little older, a little greyer, a little heavier but Carl remembered her face.

"Mom," Meghan said. "these two detectives are here to see you." Meghan stood at the door to the kitchen.

"Oh!" Betty answered, surprised. "What can I do for you, Detectives?" Betty asked, taking her glasses off and setting them down on the kitchen table. "Is something wrong?"

The two detectives introduced themselves to Betty.

"We're here to discuss the murder of Charlotte Davis." Steve said.

"Oh, my!" Betty said as if in shock. She sat back in her chair. "That was almost twenty-years ago. All I know if that the murderer was never found."

"That's why we're here," Carl said. "We're hoping you might be able to remember anything from that night."

"Well, I remember it being very early in the morning. The sirens and lights woke me up; scared me pretty bad. I thought there was a fire!" Betty said. "I was so scared!" She paused for a few moments.

"Just take your time, Ms. Eliason." Carl said.

"I remember looking out of the bedroom window. There were so many lights!" Betty continued. "I went downstairs and opened the door. It didn't take very long to realize whatever was going on was happening at Pat's house. The front door to the house was open and people in uniforms were all over the yard." She paused again and turned her head to look away from the Detectives. "Well," she finally said. "I figured at that point I needed to go over to the house and see if there was something I could do to help my friend, Pat, without knowing what was going on, I did know I needed to find out if my friend was alright."

Carl was writing down the information in his notebook as Steve asked another question.

"How long had you known the family?"

"Humm," Betty thought. "A good three-years." She said, shaking her head as if to make sure she was correct. "We moved in this house in 2000 and my Henry had his heart attack two years later, bless his heart."

"So sorry to hear that," Carl said. "So, you walked over to the Davises' house…and what happened?"

"Oh, my goodness!" Betty said. "There were people everywhere! The Officer almost didn't let me in. I told him that I was Pat's friend and I needed to be there for her."

Steve and Carl looked at each other. It was apparent that Betty Eliason had not recognized the young Officer that had been assigned to the case that night.

"Pat was crying so hard, she made me cry. She told me that Joe had found poor Charlotte lying face down in the backyard swimming pool." Betty put her head down and took a deep breath. "We went into the kitchen where we could be alone and out of the way. It was the saddest thing in the world!"

Carl and Steve slowly shook their heads in agreement.

"What can you tell us about Charlotte Davis?" Steve asked cautiously.

"Ugh!" Betty said. "Charlotte Davis. She was very sweet, don't get me wrong, very respectful to me, but as we said back in my day, a little 'fast'. She was in college you know and came home for holidays and the summer. I'd see her coming home with her boyfriend sometimes, when I was sitting out front. He had his hands all over her! We all saw it, all the time. And the way she dressed! My goodness…"

Steve interrupted. "Did you know anything about her boyfriend?"

"No." Betty said. "I know Pat was not crazy about him. She said he was a slouch. He worked in a video game shop, wore big baggy clothes, but she tolerated him because of Charlotte. Actually, my daughter could probably tell you more than me. They were great friends for a while."

Everyone turned toward Meghan.

"Charlotte was all right." Meghan said. "Just a little wild when she was with Brad."

"Do you know his last name?" Steve asked.

"Yes…Simmons."

Carl suddenly remembered that Pat had said that Charlotte had gone out with her boyfriend, Brad Simmons, and some friends the night of her murder. Carl wrote the name down and circled it.

"We went shopping together a few times and sometimes I went over to drink a little wine with her. I never went out with her friends and her. You might want to talk with JoAnna O'Neill, our next-door neighbor. They were really close." Meghan said, putting her head down. "It was awful, just awful!"

"I have to ask you, Meghan, but can you think of anyone that may have wanted to hurt Charlotte?" Carl asked.

"No, of course not." Meghan answered. "But I do know that there was a guy on her campus that wouldn't leave her alone. She said he was in one of her classes and even ended up at her dorm one night. Charlotte said he had a crush on her but she didn't want anything to do with him."

"Do you have a name?" Steve asked.

"Unfortunately, no." Meghan answered. "She never mentioned his name, just that she couldn't stand him."

"Well, that's about all for today." Steve said. "Here's my card." He said, giving Betty his business card. "If you can think of anything else, please don't hesitate to call us."

"Where are my manners?" Betty asked. "I didn't offer you a cup of coffee!"

"Next time." Carl assured her. "I'm sure there'll be a next time!"

- CHAPTER 5 -

11738 ALABASTER COURT

JoAnna O'Neill was raised in the house located at 11738 Alabaster Court, the house she would inherit from her mother who had passed away from breast cancer in 2013. Her father had passed away many years before from pancreatic cancer. The two had lived in the house for more than twenty-years, her mother occupying it when Charlotte Davis was murdered. Thirty-three-year-old JoAnna became a teacher at a local middle school in Lexington in 2014 but had been living in Raleigh, North Carolina with a former girlfriend when her mother was diagnosed with breast cancer. She took a leave of absence to care for her mother but subsequently decided to live in the house. JoAnna's girlfriend in Raleigh refused to make the move to Lexington because of her job so the two found it necessary to break up.

Melissa Edwards was a mere twenty-four-years-old when she met JoAnna O'Neill at the Singletary Center on the campus of the University of Kentucky where she worked and attended school. Melissa was selling tickets at the Center for an upcoming event that JoAnna wanted to attend. When she finally reached the ticket counter, the show had been sold out. Melissa apologized and gave JoAnna a 'rain check' for any upcoming show for the same price. The two would see each other several times at the Singletary Center and finally exchanged phone numbers and planned to have drinks at a bar near the campus. JoAnna and Melissa began to date, and in the fall of 2015, when same sex marriage was legalized in the country, were married in the back yard of JoAnna's home. The other residents of Alabaster Court were invited; most attended, a few protested the marriage altogether.

"Somebody's pulling into the driveway," Melissa said as she peeped out of the living room window. "Are you expecting anyone?"

JoAnna came into the living room and peeped out of the window as well.

"It's the same car that was at Mrs. Eliason's house this week." Melissa said. "Meghan told me that two Detectives were questioning her mother about the girl they found murdered at Mrs. Jackson's pool back in the day."

"Well, I wasn't even living here when that happened." JoAnna said, closing the curtain as the two detectives approached the front door. Steve Martinez knocked on the door and JoAnna answered it.

"Ma'am, I'm Detective Martinez and this is my partner, Detective Spenser." We just have a few questions to ask you, if you have the time."

"Oh, sure." JoAnna responded. "Come in please."

The two detectives walked into the house. Carl took out his note pad and pen to record the conversation.

"Please, have a seat." JoAnna said. "This is my wife, Melissa."

"Hello." Melissa said. "Can I offer you something to drink? Coffee?"

"No thank you." Steve said. "I assume you weren't living in this house at the time of the murder, right?"

"That's right." JoAnna answered. "This was my parents' house. My mother lived here. I inherited the house but I didn't move into it until 2014. I was living in North Carolina at the time of the murder."

"Do you know your neighbors very well?" Carl asked. "Are you particularly close to any of them?"

Melissa answered. "Mostly 'hi' and 'how are you' to everyone but we're pretty close with the Blackwell's, across the Court on the corner. We got to know them when Peter came over to unstop the toilet. He's the resident Plumber." Melissa laughed. "They hadn't been here too long so he told us about his wife, Amy. I was on my way to the grocery one day and she was outside with her two babies at the time. I pulled over to their house and introduced myself. "We've been pretty good friends ever since."

"Did you ever hear your mother talk about the night Charlotte Davis died?" Steve asked JoAnna.

"My mother called me the morning after it happened. She was very distraught. I was as well since I had grown up with her. Occasionally I've heard other people talking about Charlotte years later; how she was a bit flirtatious." JoAnna continued. "Everybody seemed to have a theory as to why she was murdered. Most people I've heard talking about it think it was her boyfriend."

"Humm." Steve said.

"Do you know Cora Jackson and her daughter, Marie, very well?" Carl asked.

"I know Marie pretty well." Melissa said. "It was so frightening when she went missing. The whole Court went gloomy! She's a good person."

"I've had a couple beers with the boys next door." JoAnna said, laughing. "I actually went over there to tell them to turn their music down in the early morning hours, and the boy that answered the door invited me in and put a beer in my hand." She continued. "We've been best buds ever since!"

"There's a couple people that don't seem to care about our arrangement over here." Melissa said bluntly. "We invited everyone to our wedding but we quickly found out who could be suffering from a bit of homophobia…"

"I'm sorry to hear that." Steve said.

"Oh, it's okay." Melissa said, shaking her head. "Most of the residents are pretty cordial."

"Well," Steve said. "Thank you so much for your time. If you can think of anything else, please give us a call." He reached in his pocket and pulled out a business card to give to Melissa.

It was the cool of the evening and the sun was slowly setting when the two detectives drove away from Alabaster Court, only to come back another day.

- CHAPTER 6 -

11735 ALABASTER COURT

T he third house on the right of the Court was a rental house, right next door to JoAnna and Melissa. Various students from around the country that attended the University of Kentucky had lived in the house for over twenty-years. To the other residents, it seemed as though new neighbors moved in and out every two-four years, once a particular group graduated from the University. The young men, and occasionally young women could be worrisome to their neighbors at times with parties, loud music and trash cans filled to the brim with beer bottles on trash collection day. Most of the time the grass was so long that onions were beginning to grow which caused a neighbor or two to contact the owner to have him threaten the inhabitants with eviction if they didn't take better care of their surroundings.

At the time of Charlotte Davis' murder in 2003, there was no one living in the rental house because of major repairs being made, it was impossible to trace any of the students that lived there or their many guests.

It was close to 10:00am when the two Detectives pulled the car into the driveway at 11735 Alabaster Court, the rental house that accommodated the young University of Kentucky students.

"I feel like I live here." Carl said. "I wouldn't be surprised if they're all asleep."

"Yeah, I remember when I was that age." Steve said. "I had chores to do or I was grounded. These kids are away from home so doing chores on a Saturday morning, even for themselves, is probably the last thing they have on their minds."

"The house looks dark." Carl said.

"Yeah, well, let's just wake 'em up!" Steve said as the two stepped out of the car and walked up the stairs to the front door. Carl reached back in the car for his note pad and pen. After several minutes of knocking on the door, a young man dressed in just pajama bottoms opened the door. He began to rub his eyes.

"Can I help you?" The young man said.

"I'm Detective Spenser and this is my partner Detective Martinez. Got a few minutes to talk with us?" Carl said.

"Is something wrong, sir?" The young man asked.

"No." Carl said. "We're investigating the murder of Charlotte Davis, happened back in 2003…"

"Hell," he said interrupting Carl. "I was born just three years before that!" He laughed as if he had told a funny joke. "You probably need to talk to Chuck. He's been here the longest. I'll go wake him up."

The young man began to walk away from the door and then suddenly came back to ask the Detectives if they would like to come inside the house.

"Yes," said Steve. "That would be nice. Thank you."

The young man ran up the stairs and after another few minutes another young man came down the stairs with pajama pants on and slipping into a tee shirt.

"Are you Chuck?" Steve asked.

"Yes, sir." He answered.

"Can we talk a bit?"

"Of course, but what is this about?" He asked, leading the way to the living room. "Please, have a seat."

"How long have you lived here?" Steve asked.

"Four years. I moved in when I was a sophomore at UK. One of my roommates found the house. It was advertised on campus; four other guys were already living here but they've since moved out and we have four new guys that took their places."

"Are you aware that a young woman was murdered just a couple of houses away from here?" Carl asked.

"Oh, yeah. Charlotte Davis." He responded with a sigh of relief that the Detectives had not come for anything to do with him personally.

"So, you know about her."

"Charlotte Davis is a cult favorite around here. There's even a poem about her… 'Charlotte Davis was found dead in her pool; bashed in the head with an unknown tool. Oh! What are we gonna' do? Charlotte Davis has lost her shoe…'"

"That's enough, son." Carl said.

"Sorry." The young man said. "I didn't mean any disrespect. Everybody says it."

"How many of you live here now?" Steve asked.

"There's six of us here now but people move in and out of here all of the time. I've been here the longest, working on my Master's Degree."

"Where are you from, son?" Carl asked.

"Indiana, sir."

"What are you studying?" Carl continued.

"Working on my MBA. Then I'll go back home and open up my own business. Don't know what kind yet…"

"Can you tell us anything about Charlotte Davis that you may have heard over the years?" Carl asked.

"Just that she was hot, and didn't mind showing it. I heard she used to lay out by her pool, hardly nothing on. But that's all I've ever heard about her."

"Okay then." Steve said. "I think we've got all we can get from here. Sorry to wake you up."

"No problem." The young man said. "Time to get up anyway." He yawned and stretched.

"Well, thanks a lot for your help." Steve said. As usual, he reached in his pocket and gave him a business card. "Call if you can think of anything else."

"But of course!"

Once inside the car, Carl started to laugh.

"A cult following?" He said. "A song? What are these people thinking of? This was a human being that died a brutal death and someone's writing songs about her!"

"Young kids." Steve said.

"I just wonder which one of these residents has kept the story going like this?"

"Well." Steve said. "We've still got four more houses to visit. Surely one of these houses is hiding a secret!"

- CHAPTER 7 -

11732 ALABASTER COURT

David and Lori McKenzie with their two teenagers in 2003; Alex sixteen-years-old and Katie fourteen-years-old, had moved into the fourth house on Alabaster Court just about one year or so before the murder of Charlotte Davis. Their house was located next door to the Jackson's whose daughter, Marie, had been missing a short time ago. David was an Attorney with a firm downtown and Lori was a Nurse in one of the hospitals in Lexington. David and Lori moved into the house from their first home, an apartment across town. When the house at 11732 Alabaster Court went up for sale, the McKenzie's put their bid in and were excited to move in quickly. Before long they had met the majority of their neighbors and established some friendships.

It was pretty obvious that young Alex had developed a crush on the twenty-two-year-old Charlotte whom he enjoyed watching sunbathe in her pool from his back yard. Any interactions he happened to have with Charlotte were kept to friendly conversations about the families or gaming systems that he was surely addicted to. Charlotte was always kind to Alex, more than likely feeding his teenage desire for the young woman. Alex especially enjoyed spying on Charlotte when she had friends over to enjoy a beautiful summer day swimming in the pool. He imagined himself in the midst of the people at her house enjoying the attention she would be giving him.

Katie, on the other hand, enjoyed her music and jumping on her trampoline with her friends. She also enjoyed making money when she babysat for a young couple that had a two-year-old. That couple also lived in one of the apartment buildings just outside of the Court. Katie had met them when taking a walk down Alabaster Drive with a friend. The couple had a baby girl and a puppy that they were taking for a walk. Katie stopped to pet the puppy and peek at the baby in the stroller. The mother and Katie saw each other often on Alabaster Drive and she finally asked Katie if she would be interested in babysitting their daughter. Katie was very excited and after getting permission from her parents, began sitting for the child, and the puppy, when the parents went grocery shopping or to the movies.

Katie had seen her brother spying on Charlotte and teased that she was going to tell her. Alex simply ignored her and told her she was crazy.

Alex was thirty-three-years-old in 2020 and unmarried. He was a very quiet man that made a good living working for himself as a house painter. Katie, on the other hand, married a firefighter. The two bought a house not too far from their parents and had two children.

Carl honked the car horn outside of Steve's apartment to let him know that he was waiting for him. It was late afternoon on a Monday when the two made their way back to Alabaster Court.

"Man, I think this car could make its way to Alabaster Court all by itself!" Carl said to Steve. "I feel like I'm there more than I'm at my own house."

"I know what you mean." Steve answered. "We're at the McKenzie's today. If we keep up this pace, we should be finished with these interviews sometime this week."

"Yeah, and we haven't got a clue yet as to who killed Charlotte Davis, except maybe her boyfriend." Carl said.

"Once we gather all of the information we can from the families in the Court, we'll see if we can build a case against him." Steve said.

"Actually," Carl replied. "the boyfriend sounds too easy to me. From what we know so far, he's still in town with a family and a steady job. When we interviewed him the day after the murder, he said he had dropped Charlotte off at home and gone on home himself. Unfortunately for him, his parents were asleep so they couldn't corroborate his story. He was on the radar for years after but he never was in any kind of trouble. This case has baffled me and a whole bunch of other people…welcome to the club!"

Carl drove the car down Alabaster Drive and into the Court. He pulled the car into the driveway at 11732. He took the note pad and pen out of his jacket and followed Steve to the front door. Steve rang the doorbell and David McKenzie answered the door.

"Can I help you?" He said.

"David McKenzie?" Steve asked.

"Yes. What can I do for you?" David asked.

"I'm Detective Martinez and this is my partner, Detective Spenser." Steve said. "Do you mind if we come in for a few minutes?"

"May I ask what this is about?"

"We're investigating the death of Charlotte Davis, 2003. We have just a few questions for you." Carl said trying to ease David's mind.

"My family has already told the police everything we know. That was a long time ago; I don't even know if I remember much."

"Well, whatever you remember will be fine." Carl said.

David looked around for a moment or two and finally shook his head and opened the door to let the Detectives in.

"Thank you." Carl said as the they walked into the living room.

"Have a seat." David said. "Like I said, I don't know how much help I can be. It was a long time ago."

"Well, maybe some questions can refresh your memory." Steve said. "Where were you the night of the murder?"

"My wife and I were in bed…it was the middle of the night when all hell broke out. There were lights everywhere. We didn't find out that Charlotte had been killed until the next day."

"Who told you that she was dead?" Steve asked.

"Oh man!" David said. "It was all over the place but if I'm not mistaken, the kids told us."

"Where is your wife now?" Carl asked.

"Out back watering the flowers."

"Do you think we could speak with her as well?" Steve asked.

David walked to the back of the house and called for his wife, Lori. She came inside wiping her hands on a paper towel with a perplexed look on her face.

"These two Detectives are investigating Charlotte Davis' murder."

"Oh dear." Lori said sitting down. "This again? Over the years we've had to answer all sorts of questions. I don't think we can help any more than we have already."

"How long have you been living here?" Steve asked.

"About a year-and-a-half before that poor girl was murdered." Lori said. "I still think about it sometimes. Her poor parents!"

"Our two children were teens at the time. They've been questioned as well. David said. "Our son, Alex, was questioned as if he was a suspect because he knew her a little more than any of us did."

"And, where was he?" Steve asked.

"In his room." David said. "He was playing one of his games when Lori told the kids to get dressed. Everyone thought there was a fire somewhere in the Court."

"How well did you know Charlotte and her family?" Carl asked.

"I knew the Davises well enough to say hello. They were pretty private. Most of their friends came from outside of the Court." Lori said. "Now Charlotte, on the other hand, was a party girl. We can see their backyard from our deck in the back and she was nothing less than wild when she was at home from school. All those kids out there at their pool! And that boyfriend of hers; trash! Be sure to question him!"

"Where are your children now?" Steve asked.

"Well," David answered. "Alex is probably just getting home by now. He's a painter, has his own business. Katie is a Nurse, like her mother, at work until 11pm tonight but her hours stagger during the week."

"We'll need their addresses and phone numbers." Steve said.

"They were kids back then and may have seen or heard something that they shared between each other and didn't say anything to the parents."

David and Lori looked at each other for a moment.

"I suppose we have to cooperate!" Lori said sarcastically.

Carl tore a sheet of paper from his note pad and gave it to Lori. She wrote the addresses and phone numbers down and gave the sheet of paper back to Carl.

"Thank you." He said.

"Do you have a business card, a number where we can reach you if we can remember anything else?" David asked.

Steve reached in his pocket and brought out another business card and gave it to Lori.

"Well," Carl said. "thank you for your time."

David walked the two Detectives to the door.

"Thank you for your time." Steve said. The Detectives walked quietly to the car, once inside Steve said,

"Boy, she sure was cross, wasn't she?"

Carl agreed, shaking his head. "Probably tired of being questioned. We'll see what will come of the conversation with the kids."

Carl backed the car out of the driveway at 11732 knowing that in just a few hours ahead, he and Steve would be right back here at Alabaster Court.

- CHAPTER 8 -

11729 ALABASTER COURT

Cora Jackson, a single mother forty-three-years-old in 2020 with one daughter, Marie eighteen-years-old, lived with Cora's father at 11729 Alabaster Court. The house that they lived in is also a rental house, the one owned by Mr. and Mrs. Joseph Davis, the parents of Charlotte Davis, the young girl that had been murdered and left in the pool in the backyard of this very house.

Cora was married to Drew Jackson and living in the deep south in 2003. After the death of their daughter, Joe and Pat Davis lived in the house for another year before putting it up for rent, retired from Toyota, left Kentucky and moved to Florida. Joe came from Florida to personally show Cora the house. He was unwavering about telling the whole story to Cora when she came to look at the house. He was particularly adamant about showing Cora the pool where Charlotte had been found. Joe's heart was still breaking but talking about it still seemed to ease a bit of the pain.

Cora had been an Administrative Assistant for Human Resources at a manufacturing company in the deep south when her husband was transferred to Lex Mark in Lexington. She was homesick and desperate to find a place to stay and luckily Cora fell in love with the Davis house and felt that the Real Estate Agency had made the best decision to send her there to take a look at the house. No one at that time told Marie that Charlotte had died in the pool.

After applying for several jobs and working temporary jobs for a while, Cora was hired as an Administrative Assistant at the Lexington Herald-Leader Newspaper office. Cora loved the job and the extra income would certainly come in handy for senior essentials that Marie was looking at during her senior year; the cost of class ring, cap and gown, and pictures to name a few items. Marie was also planning visits to the Universities that had accepted her which meant transportation, food and other necessities.

Several years after Cora moved into the Davises' house in Kentucky, her eighty-year-old father who had been diagnosed with Dementia and Cora moved him to Kentucky from the deep south to live with her and Marie. Drew had become unstable in the marriage and had many times threatened Cora with bodily harm for no apparent reason after one too many drinks. She finally grew tired of the threats, the mental abuse and the alcohol, and worried that Marie, who was now in her early teen years would be hurt by the constant arguments. Cora filed for divorce.

Drew and Cora's daughter, Marie, was an extremely intelligent young lady and became the talk of the Court when she went missing at eighteen-years-old in 2020. Because no one in the Court was certain as to what exactly had happened to Marie, the gossip ranged from her running away with someone that she had met online to her sneaking away to Las Vegas to get married or that the house was apparently a jinx to young women.

In the car again and heading toward Alabaster Court, Carl stared out of the window and began to reflect on what had occurred at the upcoming house they would be visiting that day; the home of Joe and Pat Davis, seeing Charlotte Davis lying face down in the pool, his first case as a rookie cop, now the home of Cora Jackson, mother of the missing girl case just a few weeks ago.

"Hey Carl, are you with me?" Steve asked.

"Yeah, man, I'm here." Carl answered. "Just a lot of thoughts."

Mr. Dupuis, Cora's father, was sitting in a rocking chair on the front porch enjoying the day when Carl and Steve made their way to 11729 Alabaster Court.

"Hello, Mr. Dupuis." Carl said. "Remember me?" Once again taking his note pad and pen out of his jacket. Mr. Dupuis stared at Carl, ruffling his brow as if he was struggling to remember him. "That's ok, Mr. Dupuis." Carl said. "Is Miss Cora here?"

Just then, Cora Jackson came to the door.

"I thought I heard someone talking." Cora said. Carl smiled when she opened the door and motioned for the detectives to enter. "How are you doing Detective Spenser. Good to see you!"

"Same here, Ms. Cora." Carl said. "This is my partner Detective Martinez."

"Nice to meet you. Please have a seat. Would you like some coffee?"

"Oh, no, thank you." Carl replied. "Is Marie around this afternoon?"

"Still at school, senior class rehearsal for graduation. I'll tell her that you stopped by. Are you here to check on her?" Cora asked, sitting down on the couch next to Carl.

"Of course, I'm always happy to see her, but we're actually investigating the murder of Charlotte Davis, the young woman that was murdered in your backyard back in 2003." Carl said.

Cora was quiet for a few moments. "You know I rented this house from her father, but we weren't here when it happened."

"Yes, I know." Carl answered. "We were just wondering if you had heard anything about the murder since you've been here, and also the conversation you had with Joe Davis when he came from Florida to meet you. What was that conversation like?"

"There's been lots of talk about that poor girl, good and bad." Cora said. "It was the talk of my new neighbors when we first moved in.

Everyone that stopped by to welcome us had a few words to say about the murder. A couple of them even asked if I knew that the girl had been murdered and allegedly dumped in the pool in my new backyard; talking like I didn't know."

"Did anyone talk about who they thought might have killed Charlotte Davis?" Steve asked.

"There was lots of gossip when we first moved in; mostly about her boyfriend. Most people think it was him. I also heard there was some boy at her school that liked her but she didn't like him. Some say he could have come here and when she rejected him, he murdered her. Over the years, several Detectives have stopped by to view the crime scene." Cora continued. "I'm surprised to see you here talking about a murder! Aren't you a missing persons' Detective?"

"I am." Carl replied. "I'm sort of 'on loan' to Homicide right now. I was one of the two first responding policemen on the scene that night. We're sort of backtracking, interviewing everyone in the Court to see if we can come up with some new evidence."

"I see." Cora said. "Well, I do know that Mr. Davis actually brought me to the backyard to tell me the story, the whole story. He was very emotional and he seemed as though he was reliving the whole thing all over again. He said that his wife was still so very torn up. They lived here for a year but had to move. Mr. Davis told me that they couldn't bear living in the house anymore. I knew the killer had never been arrested, but it seems to me that whoever the killer is, he wasn't after someone random; he was after Charlotte Davis in particular."

"Why do you say that?" Steve asked.

"The killer didn't go inside the house, didn't take a thing; didn't harm anyone else but Charlotte. Mr. Davis told me that the only evidence they had was the fact that one of her shoes was missing."

"That's all very true, Ms. Cora." Carl said.

"Do you mind if we take a look out back?" Steve asked.

"Oh, no, not at all." She replied. "There should be a pathway from here to the backyard with the number of investigators that have been here!" Cora laughed.

Carl thought about how different the house looked from the time that the Davises had lived there. The outside of the house itself had been painted. The backyard and the deck looked the same, except for the patio furniture and the addition of more flowers and plants. A new privacy fence had been put up and painted, and so had the deck. The two walked around the backyard for a few moments as Carl told Steve about that night in 2003 as Cora watched from the kitchen window.

"Well, thank you Ms. Cora." Steve said as he shook her hand. "Please give me a call if you hear anything or remember anything that could be helpful about this case."

"Yes, of course I will." Cora said.

"Nice to meet you," Steve said.

"Same here." She replied.

Mr. Dupuis was sound asleep in the chair on the front porch when the two Detectives came out of the house. Cora woke him up gently and led him inside.

"Have a great day." She said as she closed the front door.

Carl sighed as he got into the car and as he and Steve drove away, Carl counted the number of houses that were left to be visited.

- CHAPTER 9 -

11726 ALABASTER COURT

T he eldest couple of the residents of Alabaster Court and those that had lived the longest in the Court, resided in the house at 11726, second to the end on the left. Mark Kavanaugh and his wife, Carol, were in their early sixties when Charlotte Davis was murdered in 2003.

Mark still maintained a strong connection to the University of Kentucky as a Professor Emeritus in the English Department. Carol, on the other hand, was a stay at home mother having raised five children who were already grown and spread throughout the country in 2003. With an empty next, Carol Kavanaugh became a volunteer at the Veterans Administration Hospital. Her devotion to the veterans stemmed from her father having been a war veteran and a strong desire to assist with the care of the men and women that had served, just as her father.

Mark and Carol had seen people come and go in the Court. They were always kind to the new residents and did their best to serve as an example to their neighbors; keeping the lawn manicured and adhering to the rules and regulations of the neighborhood association. Many times, other residents sought their advice for maintaining their homes and who to call in the case of emergencies.

The Kavanaugh's were grandparents to eleven and great-grandparents to two. During the school year, the home was the quietest in the Court but summers brought the older grandchildren for alternate vacations with their grandparents and the younger ones came with their parents. During the tragedy at the Davis' home, the Kavanaugh's chose to slow the visits down during that summer since the case had not been solved. The basketball goal was the favorite of all the summertime activities that the Kavanaugh's made available for the grandchildren. There was also an above ground pool in the backyard and plenty of inside games to keep them busy.

Mark still enjoyed mowing his own grass and Carol managed a vegetable garden, growing much more than she and Mark could use for themselves. Carol could often be seen bringing cucumbers and tomatoes to Betty Eliason and Cora Jackson when the season was in. She also had a beautiful flower garden growing in the front of the house; knockout roses, daffodils, azalca bushes and mums in the fall. People in the Court could always tell what season or holiday of the year it was by the decorations at the Kavanaugh home. Whether Thanksgiving or Christmas, or just summer or spring, the Kavanaugh's home ushered in the years with colorful lights, flags, blowup characters and nativity scenes.

"Can you get away this afternoon for our second to the last interview in the Court?" Steve said to Carl. "I know you're still working on some missing persons cases but I'd like to finish these interviews before the end of the month."

"Yeah." Carl said. "But I probably need to sneak out of here. My partner is about to quit on me!"

"Just a couple more hours," Steve said. "and you'll be back in the grips of missing persons!"

"Ok," Carl replied. "But it'll have to be later this afternoon. Got some paperwork I need to finish before I can leave."

"Sounds good to me," Steve said. "Got some things over here that can keep me busy, too. I'll drive today. Pick you up at 6pm."

"Great!" Carl said. "See you then."

Steve's car seemed to float along the streets of Lexington on the way back to Alabaster Court. He pulled into the driveway at 11726. An American flag was hanging from the front door. Carl, as usual, pulled his note pad and pen out of his jacket pocket and opened the car door.

"Mark and Carol Kavanaugh, that's who we're interviewing today." Steve said.

"Alright." Carl said, ringing the doorbell at the house. "What a beautiful yard!" He continued. "So many colors."

The door opened and there stood Carol Kavanaugh.

"Yes." She said. "May I help you?"

"I'm Detective Martinez and this is my partner, Detective Spenser."

"Detectives, huh?" Carol said. "What has my husband done now?" She said laughing.

"I assure you it's not your husband." Carl said returning the laugh. "But if you do have a few minutes, we would like to talk to you and your husband about a continuing investigation, a murder that happened here, in Alabaster Court in 2003."

"Are you talking about the Davis girl that lived next door?"

"Yes, ma'am." Carl answered. "We've opened a new investigation in hopes of finding some new information about the case."

"Well, don't know how much we'll remember but…come on in."

The décor of the house was striking; crown molding, large dark furniture and a wall lined with bookshelves and books from ceiling to floor. On one of the shelves was a shadow box with an American flag folded in traditional military fashion.

"I'm sure you have some questions that'll hopefully spark some memories." Carol said, leading the way through the house. Sitting in the smaller living room on the couch was Mark Kavanaugh watching the evening News on the large screen television hanging on the wall.

"Mark, this is…what did you say your names were again?"

"Uh, Detectives Spenser and Martinez." Carl said.

"Detectives?" Mark repeated, turning the television off.

"Yes, honey. You failed to cut the grass so they're here for you!" She laughed. "Just kidding, they're here to talk about that young girl that died next door." Mark and Carol laughed together.

"Well, if we can help, we will but that was a very long time ago." Mark said. "What would you like to know?"

"First off, how long have you lived here?" Carl asked.

"Long time, 47 years or more. We've been here the longest of all of the residents of the Court." Carol said. "We moved here when Mark started teaching at the University. We raised our children here and welcomed our grandchildren."

"And we've seen people come and go all these years." Mark added.

"What do you remember about that night?" Steve asked.

"The lights woke us up." Mark said. "There were lights and vehicles all over the court; in our driveways, and up and down Alabaster Drive. We went to the living room window but the way our house faces, we couldn't tell which house it was."

"It wasn't until the next day that we found out it was Joe and Pat Davis' girl that had actually been murdered." Carol added, putting her hand on her heart.

"How did you find out?" Steve asked.

"Detectives." Mark said. "Detectives were asking questions just like you're doing the next few days to follow. And then they came back again almost every other year asking questions. I'm sure it was to help solve the case. But…the killer was never found."

"Did you know much about Charlotte…the Davises' daughter?" Carl asked.

"I saw her sometime, when I went to her house to drop off vegetables from my garden for her family. She was very respectful to me, but I can't say the same for those friends of hers." Carol said. "They were loud late at night. We could hear them at the pool. And if I remember correctly, there was a boyfriend…I think I may have met him once or twice. He just didn't seem like the kind of boy her parents would have wanted for her."

"Why do you say that?" Steve asked.

"I'm not sure, actually…they just didn't look good together, if you know what I mean. He wore baggie pants and tee shirts, tattoos everywhere, like a hoodlum, and she was always dressed to the nines. I just never felt good about the two of them." Carol answered.

"I see." Steve responded. "Well, here's my card. Call if you can think of anything else that might be helpful."

Carol took the business card from Steve and laid it on the coffee table.

Mark stood to shake the Detectives hands and walked with Carol to the front door.

"This is a beautiful house." Carl said, looking around. "I see you have a military flag on your bookshelf. A family member?"

"Yes." Carol said. "My father was an Army retiree; a war veteran. I was an Army brat, as they say. He died many years ago, buried in Arlington National Cemetery. Dad was buried twelve-feet and mom was buried on top of him when she passed fourteen years later. I always felt like I needed to do something for the veterans so I volunteer at the local Veterans Administration Hospital three days each week."

"That's just wonderful." Carl said excited. "What do you do at the hospital?"

"Anything they need." Carol continued. "Make coffee, visit patients, run errands…I just love being there with the Veterans."

"And while she spends her time with other men, I'm working on her 'honey do' lists!" Mark added with a haughty laugh.

"Don't let him fool you, Detectives!" Carol joked. "He's surrounded by a lecture hall at the University full of beautiful young girls!"

They both laughed.

"Well." Steve said. "Time to hit the road. We sincerely thank you for your time and input into this case. Be sure to call if you think of anything else."

"We certainly will." Mark said, standing at the door to the house. He began to wave as the Detectives got back into the car. Carol joined him.

"It was like visiting family." Carl said.

"Yep." Steve answered. "I felt the same way. In fact, my grandparents are just like them…laughing and joking around all the time. Carol had no use for Charlotte's boyfriend, did she?"

"Absolutely not!" Carl answered matter-of-factly. "None of the people we've interviewed seem to have any love for Brad. Supposedly he loved her so much; why would he kill her?"

"I don't know." Steve answered. "One more house and then we'll play catch-up with the McKenzie kids and Brad Simmons,

CHAPTER 10

11723 ALABASTER COURT

Peter and Amy Blackwell were not only the youngest couple in the Court but had lived there the least amount of time. The house itself had been left unoccupied for several years, and had been up for sale as a 'fixer upper' when the Blackwell's looked into purchasing it.

Prior to moving to Alabaster Court, both were living in a rental house that was suddenly too small with the expectance of their third child.

Peter was a professional plumber that worked for a well-established company in Lexington and made a good living for the family. He was also helpful to his neighbors who needed his plumbing expertise at times, including the University of Kentucky students that lived across the Court who were frequently facing a stopped-up sink or garbage disposal problems.

Amy worked part-time as a Cashier at Joseph Beth Booksellers in Lexington Green while the children were in day care. She had become friends with Marie Jackson who babysat for the Blackwell's so that they could sometimes enjoy some adult time. Marie would also just stop by sometime for a visit with the children which would give Amy the opportunity to make a quick grocery store run. She became extremely distraught when Marie went missing and did her best to console Cora Jackson.

The two had become friends with JoAnna and Melissa who also lived across the Court, playing cards or watching movies together when time permitted. Melissa was eager to have a child and showered the Blackwell's children with love and plenty of attention. She shared her desire with Amy who was always ready to listen to her and offer her advice as well. JoAnna also wanted a child but was much more patient about waiting for a donor.

Peter and Amy Blackwell were sitting outside in the front of their house with their three little girls when Carl and Steve drove up to 11723 Alabaster Court. It was the cool of the evening after a beautiful, sunny day. One little girl, seemingly the oldest, was riding a tricycle on the sidewalk with the assistance of her dad; the middle girl was in a child sized swimming pool while the baby was sitting on her mother's lap on the porch. Carl pulled the car along the side of the curb to avoid interrupting the pathway the oldest girl was riding on her trike.

"Is this the Blackwell house?" Steve asked as he exited the car.

"Yes, it is." The man said. "Can I help you?"

"Good evening. I'm Detective Martinez and this is my partner Detective Spenser. Do you have a few minutes to answer some questions?"

"What kind of questions?" Peter said. By this time, Amy had taken the older girl and the tricycle to the driveway.

"We are re-opening the case of the murder of Charlotte Davis that happened here at Alabaster Court in 2003." Steve said.

"Oh, yeah!" Amy yelled out. "Melissa told me that you guys had questioned them about that." She said as she walked closer to her husband with the baby on her hip. "We've only been here less than five years so we really don't know anything about it."

"We understand that," Steve said. "but have you heard anything about the case at all?"

"Well, just what Marie has said." Amy continued. "She said it scares her sometimes at night, knowing that she might be sleeping in the very same room that the poor girl might have slept in."

"Do you mean Marie Jackson? The young girl that recently went missing?" Carl asked. He took out his note pad and pen, and began to take notes.

"Yes." Amy said. "She babysits for our girls sometimes. We were so worried about her when she went missing. She's a really sweet girl. I went over to Mrs. Jackson's house to see if there was anything I could do to help her. She was so very sad. I could truly understand why Marie felt uncomfortable in that house. It was just eerie knowing that someone was murdered there."

"We've heard all of the gossip and the theories around here about her death but we've pretty much ignored it since we weren't here when it happened." Peter said.

"What kind of theories?" Steve asked.

"Oh, just that the McKenzie's boy might have had something to do with it." Peter said. "It's big time gossip that he had a mad crush on her and she saw him as a little boy."

"I see." Steve said, looking at Carl. "Thank you for your time."

"No problem." Peter said.

Back inside of the car again, Carl began to review the notes he had on the McKenzie interview.

"Time to visit the McKenzie kids!" He said.

"Yeah…" Steve responded. "Next on the list."

- CHAPTER 11 -

ALEX AND KATIE

Katie McKenzie-Boyd slowly made her way home after a long night-shift at one of the local hospitals in Lexington. It was a chilly morning and as she walked toward her front door, she pulled her sweater around her shoulders and shivered. She quietly opened the door, not to awaken her husband and children and walked directly to the coffee pot that was automatically brewing the precious decaf that she desperately needed to warm up.

Across town, Detective Steve Martinez dialed Detective Carl Spenser on his phone and patiently waited for him to answer.

"Time to get up, sleepy head." Steve said to Carl when he finally answered the call.

"What time is it?" Carl asked, stretching.

"8:00am, my brother. Time to get up." Steve teased. "We need to be at the Boyd residence before Katie goes to bed. Remember? She said 9:00am."

"I'll be there in forty-five minutes so get up and make yourself decent." Steve said.

"I'm on it!" Carl said, climbing out of bed. He quickly showered and grabbed a cup of black coffee and his usual toast with strawberry jam. Minutes later, Steve honked the horn.

"Tell me again why we agreed to meet with Katie early on a Saturday morning?" Carl asked.

"She works nights all week and off on Saturday. She can stay up a little later on Saturday which is why she suggested we stop by this morning." Steve answered.

Steve drove the car through the community as Carl searched the mailboxes for the correct street number.

"There it is." Carl said, pointing to the Boyd house.

Steve pulled into the driveway and the two Detectives got out of the car. Carl made sure he had his note pad and pen in tow. Before Steve could knock, Katie McKenzie-Boyd opened the door still dressed in her scrubs. She looked extremely tired but smiled as she led the way to the kitchen.

"My family is still asleep and the kitchen is the furthest room from the bedrooms." Katie said. "I hope you don't mind. Have a seat please. Would you like some coffee?"

"Just had some, thanks." Carl said. Steve smiled and shook his head no.

"What kind of work does your husband do?" Carl asked.

"He's a Firefighter. So…you have some questions about the Charlotte Davis murder?" Katie asked.

"Yes," Steve said. "And we appreciate you meeting with us."

"No problem." She said, yawning. "Excuse me!"

"How old were you when the incident in 2003 happened?" Steve asked.

"I was fourteen-years-old. My parents bought the house just one-year or so before Charlotte Davis was found dead."

"Did you know her very well?" Carl asked.

"Not really. She was a lot older than me." Katie said. "I did see her and her friends when I was outside in our backyard. I had a trampoline in those days that I stayed on. We could see her backyard from ours."

"What do you remember about that night?" Steve asked.

"Uh!...I'm not sure what woke me up; the sirens coming into the Court or the lights. There were so many lights! I yelled out for my mom and she came running in my room. She thought it was a fire at first. She told me to get dressed. Then she went into my brother's room and told him the same thing. Evidently, one way or another my dad realized it wasn't a fire and told us to stay in the house. He went on the porch to try to find out what had happened."

"And when did you find out what had happened?" Steve asked.

"I'm not sure." Katie answered. "My dad came in and said he saw vehicles out there in the Court. My mom just hugged me and Alex, my brother. I think they tried their best to keep it from us. I did know Charlotte wasn't there anymore and the parties weren't happening anymore."

"Do you know anything about her boyfriend?" Steve asked.

"I'd see her kissing a boy by the same car a few times in the front of the house. I guess that was him." Katie said. "He was thug looking; baggy clothes, long hair. You could tell when he drove in the Court! Sounded like he needed a muffler. I never had any conversation with him. You can probably get a lot more information from my brother, Alex. He was crazy about Charlotte." She laughed. "I used to tease him about it all the time and threatened to tell her. It made him so mad."

"Other than the trampoline, how did you spend your time?" Carl asked.

"I used to babysit for the Carlisle's that lived in the apartment buildings on the next street from the Court. I would sit for their little girl when they went out or shopping. Not much more than that. My parents didn't let me get too far away from them!"

"You're a Nurse, right?" Carl asked.

"Yes." Katie answered. "A Pediatric Nurse. From what I heard Charlotte was studying to become a Nurse or Social Worker at the time of her death. So very sad."

"Well, Katie. We do appreciate your time. I think we have enough for now. If you can think of anything else, give us a call." Steve said as he reached in his jacket pocket for a business card.

"You're certainly welcome." Katie said, taking the card. "But like I said, my brother could probably give you more information."

"We'll definitely be in touch with him as well. Thank you for your time." Carl said.

Katie walked the two Detectives to the door. They got in the car and drove away.

"Did you call Alex, too, to set up an appointment?" Carl asked.

"No, actually, I figured we could just drive over there. I knew Katie was a Nurse and worked nights but I don't have any restrictions for Alex."

Alex McKenzie, or 'Mack' as his friends called him, was sitting on the front porch of his apartment building as though he already knew that the Detectives were on their way. He looked as though he had just awakened.

"Alex McKenzie?" Steve asked.

"Yeah. That's me." Alex said, running his fingers through his hair. "What can I do for you?"

"Detectives Martinez and Spenser. We have a few questions to ask you about the Charlotte Davis murder that happened in 2003. Do you have a few minutes?" Steve asked.

"Yeah, sure." Alex answered. It was obvious that he was not going to invite the two Detectives into his apartment. Steve became extremely business-like.

"What can you tell us about the night Charlotte Davis was murdered?" Steve said very matter-of-factly.

Alex paused for a few moments, staring at the ground and then responded to the question.

"I was awake, in my room playing my game when the noise came; so many sirens and lights everywhere!" Alex said, fidgeting. "I remember my mom coming in and telling me to get dressed. My parents thought there was a fire somewhere in the Court."

"And Charlotte…what kind of a relationship did you have with Charlotte?"

Steve asked.

"I didn't have a relationship with her." Alex said agitated. "I knew who she was, we spoke when we saw each other but that's about all."

"What did you talk about when you 'spoke' to each other?" Steve asked.

"Just about playing the games or the weather, the family. Nothing much. She was older than me." Alex said.

"Did you know her boyfriend at all?" Steve asked.

"I knew who he was. I would see them kissing or playing around when I was playing basketball out front. She also had a lot of guys and girls that went over to swim in the pool." Alex responded.

"Did it make you angry or frustrated when you saw Charlotte with her boyfriend or her friends?" Steve asked.

"Why would it?" Alex asked quickly.

"Oh, I don't know. Young teenaged boy, young attractive older woman…" Steve answered.

"It wasn't like that!" Alex said angrily.

"Ok, then how was it?" Steve asked.

"Just like I said…we 'spoke' to each other." Alex said, calming down. "She was a nice person. She was nice to me. I hated hearing all of the bad things they said about her just because she liked to have fun and had lots of friends. I've heard her called a 'party girl', and things a lot worse than that. Did you know she was studying to be a Nurse? My mom's a Nurse, so is my sister. I heard very little about that or any of the other good things that she did."

"Did you have a crush on her? Were you in love with her?" Steve asked.

"Of course not." Alex answered quickly. "I just thought she was a good person. I know you've been talking with my sister. She always teased me about having a crush on Charlotte, but it wasn't like that at all."

"You just liked to watch her and her friends outside in the backyard, in their swimsuits…or less than that." Steve continued.

"I was a teenager." Alex said. "Nothing wrong with looking."

"Have you heard anything about the student in Jacksonville that did have a crush on her?" Steve asked.

"Yeah. I've heard it all…over the years. But I don't know anything about him at all, just that he was crazy about her." Alex said. "I don't know if he ever came here or not, just heard the gossip."

"Ok then." Steve said. "Nice to meet you, Alex. Here's my business card. If you can think of anything that might help this investigation, just give me a call."

"By the way," Carl added. "Did you paint the Davis' house? I noticed it was a different color."

"Yeah. I painted it." Alex said. "Does that make me a suspect?"

"Thanks, man." Carl said. "Thanks for your help."

The two Detectives walked back to the car and got in. As Steve drove away, Carl commented about the young man sitting on the front porch.

"Sounds like the perfect suspect to me."

"Speaking of suspects, we still need to interview Charlotte Davis' boyfriend…"

"Brad Simmons." Carl interrupted. "Let me get Sheila on his whereabouts. I'm sure he was interviewed several times over the years. I'll check with you as soon as I find out anything."

Chapter 12

Brad Simmons

"Hey, Sheila." Carl said over the phone. "I'm on my way in. I need you to see if you can find any information on a Brad Simmons, Charlotte Davis' boyfriend during the time of her murder. There should be information on him from previous interviews. If I remember correctly, the Homicide Detective was a Matt Parker. Check it out for me, please."

By the time Carl made it to Missing Persons the following day, Sheila was already on the job.

"Bradley J. Simmons, forty-two years old; married to Regina Carlton Simmons; 235 Sycamore Drive here in Lexington." Sheila said as Carl walked up to her desk. "The last interview he had was about ten-years ago and that's the last information we have on him."

"Excellent!" Carl said to Sheila. "Thank you so much…"

"Are you getting any closer to solving this case?" Sheila asked.

"Well, we've interviewed just about everyone except this Simmons guy. Hopefully we can catch up with him." Carl said. "Any idea where he worked or works?"

"Ten-years ago he was working for the local Newspaper Office in the Printing department. Chances are he might still be there." Sheila responded as she read through the information sheet she had just printed.

"Perfect!" Carl said excited, reaching for his phone. Sheila leaned over the desk and gave him the printout.

"Hey Martinez…got some ten-year-old news about Brad Simmons. When can we get together to check it out?"

"Tomorrow afternoon works for me." Steve answered.

"Okay, then." Carl answered. "Let's say about 2:30?"

"Works for me." Steve said. "I'll pick you up."

The two hung up the phone.

"I'll be gone tomorrow afternoon around 2:30. Hope we can find this joker." Carl said. "Ya know, it'll be good to get back to finding missing people rather than looking for a needle in a haystack."

"No leads yet?" Sheila asked.

"We haven't really put the information together yet to develop any theories but I feel good about the work we've done so far." Carl answered.

"What do you think is different about what you're doing now as opposed to what other Detectives have done so far?"

"Ten-years." Carl answered. "Can you believe it? It's been ten years since anyone looked at this case."

The day went by quickly as Carl threw himself into his daily routine in the Missing Persons Department; reports, following leads to missing persons and returning phone calls that were long overdue.

Morning came quickly as well bringing with it the signs of the summer to come. Carl stretched as he walked outside his house and to the car as his mind wandered from Missing Persons to Homicide Cold Case. Steve drove up to the Police Station and made the call to Carl to let him know that he was outside.

"See you in the morning." He said to Sheila.

"You be careful out there." She responded.

"Yep. Will do!" Carl said as he made his way through the department. He hurried out the door and into Steve's waiting car.

"We're going to either 235 Sycamore Drive or to the newspaper office. Since its mid-afternoon, I suggest the newspaper office." Carl said.

"Let's do it!" Steve said as he turned the car around and headed for the local newspaper office. Once inside, Steve introduced himself and Carl and then asked the woman at the Information Desk where he could find Bradley J. Simmons.

"He's in Printing. I can have him come to the front if you'd like." She said.

"Yes." Steve said. "That would be perfect."

Moments later, a man with a neat haircut, and clean shaven came to the Information Desk.

"Bradley J. Simmons?" Steve asked.

"Yes, sir." The man answered, curiously. "Is there something I can do for you?"

"Is there somewhere we can talk in private?"

"Yes, sir." Brad answered. "Over here." Pointing to a small room just off the Information Desk.

"Sir down, please." Steve said.

"What is this about?" Brad asked.

"We're re-opening the murder of Charlotte Davis from 2003. Was she your girlfriend during that time?"

Brad put his head down and took a deep breath.

"Yes, sir. We were together for about three years. Started dating when she was about nineteen."

"Where did you meet her?"

"Through a mutual friend from the University, Sarah Witherspoon. I told all of this to the Detectives…"

"That was a long time ago," Steve said. "Like I said, we're 're-opening' the case. What kind of a relationship did you have with Charlotte Davis?"

"I loved her and she loved me." Brad said. "But like I said, that was almost twenty-years ago. I have a wife and a child now…"

"Where were you the night she was murdered?"

"We had gone out to a house party." Brad said." "I drank a little bit too much and had one of our friends drive us home. He dropped her off first and then he dopped me off at home."

"What time was that?"

"About 1:30am."

"Can anybody verify your whereabouts?" Steve asked.

"My parents were home but they were asleep."

"So, nobody can account as to where you were at 3:00am?"

"No, sir." Brad answered. "I guess not."

"How did you find out that Charlotte was dead?" Steve asked.

"The Detective, the next day, came to question me." Brad answered. "He told me."

"Detective Matt Parker?"

"I guess that was him. I really don't remember."

"Did you kill Charlotte Davis?" Steve asked point blank.

"NO!" Brad answered, standing up. "Of course, I didn't kill her! I loved her. I was at home, in a drunken sleep! I used to do that…"

"Sit down, please!"

The room was suddenly quiet. Brad sat down and put his hand up against his forehead.

"I didn't kill her." Brad said calmly. "And I don't know who did. I had a bad reputation in those days but I've changed."

"And Charlotte?" Steve asked.

"She was a little wild, I knew that, but I was as well." Brad said. "All we wanted to do in those days was to have a good time with our friends."

"Are you positive you don't know of anyone that might have killed or wanted to kill Charlotte Davis?"

"No." Brad said softly. "I have no idea. I know that none of our friends would have done something like that."

"Well." Steve said. "That's all we have for now. Don't leave town! We may need to question you again. Are you still at 235 Sycamore Drive?"

"Yes, sir." Brad answered.

"You can go." Steve said matter-of-factly. "Thank you for your time. Here's my card if you can think of anything else."

"Yes, sir." Brad said as he walked away.

"Boy! You were really rough on him." Carl said as the two drove away from the newspaper office.

"Perhaps, but he was a suspect seventeen-years-ago and as far as I'm concerned, he still is!"

"Now that we've interviewed Brad Simmons, perhaps we can get together and leaf through some of this evidence and come up with a suspect list."

"Let's make it Friday. Steve said. "I need a break from this case! I'll call you."

BOOK II
Cora Jackson

- CHAPTER I -

MEETING

"Come on, Cora," Leslie Dupuis said to her sister. "You've been in the house too long! All you do is work and sleep. Let's go to the Jazz Festival. Who knows, you might meet somebody new."

"I'm just fine working and sleeping, and as far as meeting somebody new, I don't have the time," Cora answered sarcastically.

"Then just come with me to listen to the music." Leslie continued. "I promise I'll never bother you again!"

"I don't believe that for a minute." Cora said. "But, you're probably right. My life is just the office and the bed. I'll go for one hour."

"Make it two!"

"Don't push your luck!" Cora said as she walked toward her bedroom. "Now, to find something to wear!"

"It's going to be so hot and humid out there. I'm doing shorts and a tank top." Leslie said. "You know, with some cute heels!"

The two sisters began to laugh as they combed through Cora's clothes closet. By the time they agreed on what Cora would wear, the time was growing short for the two to get ready to go to the Jazz Festival.

"I'll pick you up in an hour." Leslie said as she headed toward the front door of Cora's apartment. "Please don't change your mind!"

"Go girl! I'll see you in an hour…and not a minute more!"

Leslie returned to Cora's apartment within the hour and was surprised to see Cora dressed and ready to go.

"Don't forget to bring a lawn chair. Don't forget to bring money to eat! I love the food at the Jazz Festival."

The two sisters traveled several miles outside of town to the place where the Jazz Festival would be held. Grabbing their lawn chairs and locking the car door, they walked to the seating area not too far from the stage but close enough to the food court.

"Isn't this great?" Leslie asked, relaxing in her lawn chair.

"Just peachy!" Cora answered as she unfolded her lawn chair and leisurely sat down.

Within a few moments, the first band made their way to the stage and began to tune their instruments. The entire area where the Jazz Festival was being held was filled with people sitting in their lawn chairs.

"Hungry yet?" Leslie asked. "You look so relaxed. I'll go get the food. What do you want?"

"I'd love a Taco Salad. I saw the advertisement on the Food Court marquee. Something sort of healthy!"

"Forget healthy!" Leslie said laughing. "Girl, we're out here to have a good time." She walked toward the Food Court, weaving in and out of people coming in to the seating area. After several long minutes, Leslie began to make her way back to their seats with the food. The first band had already begun to play. The crowd roared with excitement while several couples danced in the grass.

"Here ya go!" Leslie said, handing the Taco Salad over to Cora. "Sounded good so I got one, too."

Suddenly, two men walked up to the space where Cora and Leslie were seated. One walked directly over to Leslie and gave her a long hug.

"Darrell!" She shouted with a bright smile. "What are you doing here?"

The young man stepped back to look her up and down.

"You look wonderful!" He said. "It's been a long time."

"Where have you been? I haven't seen you around since we graduated from high school." Leslie said, still smiling.

"I took a job in town working for a local bank. I'm a Teller."

"Awesome!" Leslie said. Oh, by the way, this is my sister Cora Dupuis…Cora, this is Darrell. We went to high school together."

"Nice to meet you, Darrell." Cora said, extending her hand.

"Nice to meet you as well." He replied. "And this is my Uncle, Drew Jackson."

Drew leaned over to shake Cora's hand.

"You have some great seats here." Darrell said. "Perfect view of the stage!"

"Is that your way of asking if you can join us?" Leslie asked.

"Well, it would be nice to have some good company while we enjoy the music. Do you mind?"

"Of course not." Leslie answered. "You don't mind, do you Cora?"

"Uh…no…yes, please join us." Cora said, eyes glaring at Leslie.

The two men opened their lawn chairs and placed them strategically close to the two girls. Darrell immediately turned his attention to Leslie and the two began a private conversation while Cora turned her attention to the stage where the music was playing.

"This is a little awkward." Drew whispered, while staring at the stage.

"Yes. I would say that it is." Cora replied, as she stared at the stage as well.

"Do you like Jazz?" Drew asked, trying desperately to break the ice.

"Yes, actually I do."

"What kind of work do you do?" He asked while still staring at the stage.

"I'm an Administrative Assistant for the Tex Corporation." She answered, also still staring at the stage. "What kind of work do you do?"

"I work for IBM." He replied. "I'm a Systems Engineer."

"That sounds exciting."

"Would you like to dance?" Drew asked, extending his hand.

"Oh…me? No, thank you." Cora said smiling.

"I promise I won't bite!" Drew said, teasing.

Cora began to laugh. "I'm sure you won't." She answered.

"So, would you like a glass of wine?"

"Yes, that sounds good. Red, please."

"Okay. I'll be right back." Drew leaned over to Darrell and told him that he was going to the Food Court for wine and asked if he wanted to go with him. Darrell agreed and the two men walked toward the Food Court.

"I could break your neck!" Cora said furiously. "How could you just dump this man on me?"

"Listen. He's a great guy." Leslie pleaded her case. "I was just talking with Darrell about him. He's a widower; wife died two years ago, ovarian cancer. No children. He's the appropriate age, has a great job and is certainly easy on the eyes. Come on; give yourself a chance to the possibilities."

"Possibilities? I just met the man and you're already talking about possibilities!"

"Aw, come on, Cora!" Leslie said. "I just want you to give yourself the chance to be happy. You're right; it might not be Drew but at least you need to see where this is going."

The two girls continued to discuss the situation until Leslie saw the two men on their way back from the Food Court with two bottles of wine and four plastic wine glasses in their hands. Sitting down again, Drew opened a bottle of wine and poured some in one of the glasses and gave it to Cora.

"Thanks." She said, smiling.

"Maybe you'll dance with me after a glass of wine." Drew whispered.

Cora couldn't help but laugh at the comment.

"I can tell you find it hard to get a 'no' for an answer." Cora said, looking in his eyes.

"Actually, I think I truly understand now. Had a short talk with my nephew when we went for the wine. He said he talked with your sister about you. She said you're shy, and all you do is work…"

"And sleep." Cora interrupted. "Yes, that sounds just like my sister. In fact, we had that conversation earlier today. I'm just a tad upset with her that she would talk about me to someone I'm just now meeting."

"So, you and your sister didn't have a short conversation about me when we went for the wine?"

"Touche," Cora said, clinking her wine class to his. The two laughed and spent the new few hours enjoying the music and each other.

The night began to wear down and the music was now quiet. It was the time for closing lawn chairs and gathering personal items and taking the walk to the parking space. Drew and Darrell walked Cora and Leslie to their car and said their goodnights.

"It really was nice to meet you, Cora Dupuis. Would you mind if I called you?" Drew asked Cora.

"I think I would like that…Drew Jackson."

He took out a business card and wrote her number on the back. He leaned over and gave her a slight kiss on the cheek. She blushed as he opened the door to the car for her.

"Well, goodnight everyone." Leslie said as she drove away from the two men. "Did you have a good time? I think you did! After all, you said you wanted to leave in an hour and it's been more than three…I'd say that was a great time."

"Yep." Cora answered. It was a great time!"

- CHAPTER 2 -

THE FIRST DATE

Cora slipped the key into the lock on the door to her apartment just as her phone inside began to ring. She quickly opened the door, dropped her purse on the couch and ran to answer the phone.

"Hello." she said, short of breath.

"Cora?" the voice on the other end of the phone said. "Did I catch you at a bad time?"

"Oh, no, I was just rushing to get to the phone." She answered.

"No need to rush." The voice said. "I would have certainly called you back."

Cora smiled as she realized that the voice on the other end of the phone was Drew, the man she had just met at the Jazz Festival. She stepped out of her shoes and made herself comfortable on the couch.

"I just wanted to tell you how nice it was to meet you tonight." Drew said.

"I feel the same way." Cora answered, blushing. "I don't get out much anymore but it's hard to say no to my sister."

"Well, I'm glad she convinced you to come out. I don't get out much either but I always make time for a Jazz concert." Drew said. "That's my guilty pleasure."

Cora laughed. "Nice guilty pleasure! I really enjoyed the music, too. It was my first time attending the festival, and like I said, my sister forced me to go."

"And like I said, I'm glad she convinced you to come out."

"I am, too." Cora answered.

"Good, because I was going to ask you to have dinner with me sometime soon." Drew said, confidently.

Cora paused. There was an awkward silence. Finally, Drew spoke again. "I hope I didn't overstep myself already." Drew said.

"Oh no!" Cora answered. "It's just that I haven't had the time for dinner with anyone for a very long time."

"I understand that." Drew answered sincerely. "I'm not used to asking women out the first time I meet them, either."

"I believe you." Cora answered.

"Good, then let's put our 'used to bes' in the past and try something new. What do you say?" Drew asked. "I promise I'm a good guy!"

Cora paused again.

"I'm not taking no for an answer." Drew said. "I'll pester you like your sister did until I get you to agree to have dinner."

Both began to laugh.

"Okay." Cora said slowly. "I'll have dinner with you."

"Aw, that's great!" Drew said. How about Sunday evening? I know a little soul food restaurant downtown that serves the best shrimp etouffee I have ever eaten. How does that sound?"

"It sounds great." Cora said, finally relaxing.

Cora gave Drew her address and the two hung up the phone. Cora could not keep from smiling as she was getting ready for bed. She could hardly wait for morning to call her sister.

"I am so happy for you, Cora!" Leslie said the next morning when Cora told her about the conversation with Drew. "I'm proud of you for saying 'yes'." Leslie continued. "If he's anything like his nephew, I know he's a good guy."

Sunday came quickly. Cora scanned through her closet for something appropriate for a first date and settled for a sundress with matching jacket and sandals. She took a long look in her mirror, turning around to see all sides and gave herself an 'ok'. She sat in the living room and waited for Drew. The sound of the doorbell startled her. Within a second she realized that it must be Drew and gave herself one more look in the mirror in the living room and headed toward the door. She took a deep breath and smiled as she opened the door. There stood Drew with a lovely bouquet of spring flowers.

"Oh, my goodness!" Cora said as Drew gave the flowers to her. "They are beautiful. Please, come in and have a seat while I put these in water."

"I'm glad you like them. I toyed with the idea of being really corny bringing you flowers but I gave into my better self and hoped you'd enjoy the sentiment."

"Well, I do!" Cora said, putting the flowers in a vase on the coffee table. "I love them. Thank you so much!"

"You are welcome, beautiful lady." Drew said, looking Cora in her eyes. "Shall we leave? I made reservations for 6:30pm."

The two walked out of the apartment. Drew opened the passenger side door for Cora to let into his Chevrolet Malibu.

"This is a nice car!" Cora said.

"Another one of my guilty pleasures." Drew answered, smiling.

The music playing in the tape player was, of course, jazz. Drew asked Cora if the music was alright and she answered yes.

"Jazz is the perfect riding music." Cora said.

"I do like other types of music." Drew said. "I love old soul music and rhythm and blues."

"Me, too." Cora said. "Sounds like we have a few things in common."

"Yes." Drew answered. "I'm sure we'll find more things in common. I can just feel it!"

The restaurant was busy. Old soul, and rhythm and blues music piped through the speakers. The atmosphere was perfect. A waitress came to the table and asked for their drink orders.

"I'll have a glass of white Zinfandel, please." Cora said.

"I'll have the same." Drew added.

"Another one of those things we have in common?" Cora asked.

Drew laughed and shook his head. "I'm always eager to try something new."

Both ordered the Shrimp Etouffee with corn bread. Cora chose a brownie with vanilla ice cream for dessert and Drew ordered a slice of plain cheese cake.

"Wow!" Cora said. "That was delicious!"

"It always is." Drew answered. "Maybe next time we can try something else on the menu."

"Maybe." Cora said coyly.

"Well, since I maybe seeing you again I'd better make the most of tonight. Follow me." Drew said, taking Cora's hand and leading her to the Bar extension of the restaurant. He quickly found a table in a corner of the Bar and pulled out the chair for Cora to sit down.

"This place is really great." Cora said. "It's so large."

"Would you like a drink? Another white Zinfandel?"

"Sure. Thank you." Cora answered.

When the waitress came to the table, Drew ordered the wine and a glass of Bourbon for himself. Their conversation ranged from childhood dreams to current realities to goals for the future. Before either one realized it, the time had flown by.

"Oh, dear!" Cora said, looking at her watch. "It's after 11:00pm. I'm afraid it's getting late and I have an early morning tomorrow."

"You know what they say, 'time flies when you're having fun'!" Drew replied.

"Yes, and I have had a wonderful evening." Cora said, putting her hand softly on Drew' hand on the table. "But I really need to get home."

"I understand." Drew said, helping with her chair. "There's always another time."

Cora smiled.

Drew and Cora continued their conversation during the ride to Cora's apartment. Once at the apartment, Drew opened the car door for Cora and walked her to the door.

"I really had a great time, Drew, a really great time." Cora said. Drew smiled.

"Can I call you again?" Drew asked.

"Yes. I would like that."

Drew reached over and kissed Cora on her cheek.

"So would I."

- CHAPTER 3 -

THE FIRST APOLOGY

ora rolled over in her bed and turned off the alarm clock. It was 6:00am Monday. She stretched and then grabbed for her robe. The apartment was chilly. Cora shivered. Slipping her feet into her slippers, she walked toward the kitchen and flipped the 'on' button on the coffee pot. Suddenly, she danced a little jig and twirled around. It wasn't a dream! She smiled and twirled around again as the smell of coffee filled the kitchen. She thought about calling her sister, Leslie, but she was probably still asleep. Cora always woke up two hours before she had to be at work but Leslie would wake up at the last minute and rush around trying to get ready for work. But what the heck, Cora thought, as she dialed the number to her sister's phone.

"Hello," Leslie said after several rings. "Hello!"

"Get up, girl. I have lots to tell you!"

"Cora???" Leslie answered sleepily. "What time is it?"

"It's 6:15am. Get up!"

"Goodness, girl. I have another hour before I need to get up." Leslie said.

"Then you can have coffee with me as I tell you all about my date." Cora said excitedly.

Leslie jumped out of bed and slowly made it to the coffee pot. She sat down at the kitchen table as the coffee brewed.

"Leslie!" Cora shouted.

"I'm awake…I'm awake!" Leslie said.

"It was wonderful!" Cora said. "I had the best time!"

"That's great." Leslie said, waking up. "Tell me all about it."

And that Cora did; from what she wore, to the flowers, the dinner, the music and the kiss on her cheek.

"Oh, my goodness!" Leslie said, standing up in her kitchen. "When are you going to see him again?"

"I don't know. But he did ask me if he could call me again."

"I hope you said 'yes'."

"Why, yes I did!" Cora answered, giggling.

"Are you going to introduce him to dad?"

"Not yet." Cora said. "It's far too early. Besides, I don't want to hear any negativity from dad about him. Let's see where this is going first."

Cora's day at work was wonderful, filled with daydreams of the evening before and hopes for more of the same when she was caught off guard by the ringing of her desk phone.

"This is Cora Jackson. May I help you?"

"Yes. You sure can." The voice on the other side of the phone said. "Meet me for lunch."

"Drew?" Cora asked.

"Yep."

"How did you get my office number?" Cora asked.

"I simply called the firm you work for and here I am. Lunch?"

"Oh." Cora said, taken off guard. "I only have an hour."

"That's ok." Drew said. "I'll pick up lunch and we can sit outside. It's a really beautiful day."

"I guess you have everything covered. How can I say no?"

"That's what I was hoping for!"

The day was really beautiful. Cora and Drew sat outside on a park bench across the street from Cora's job and lunched on sandwiches, chips, sodas and cookies for dessert.

"You are so sweet!" Cora said to Drew.

"When can I see you again?" Drew asked. "I could see you every day of the week."

Cora smiled and lowered her head. "How about I cook dinner for us over the weekend?"

"I have to wait all the way until the weekend and it's only Monday? Drew said, teasing.

"Weekdays are rough. I usually go to bed early and get up early." Cora said.

"I understand. Dinner over the weekend is great."

"Saturday night?" Drew asked.

"Yes. That's perfect." Cora said. "But I have to get back to work now."

"I know." Drew said. "I'll call you later." He leaned over and kissed her on her cheek and walked her to the door of her office building.

The week went by quickly. Drew called Cora every night and the conversations continued as the two began to know each other better. Cora planned a nice dinner of grilled steaks, baked potatoes, salad and corn on the cob. She was very excited when the doorbell rang on Saturday evening. Cora had even bought a bottle of Bourbon and coke. The evening went by smoothly and as the two of them enjoyed a drink after dinner, Cora's phone rang.

"Excuse me, Drew." Cora said as she answered the phone. "Hello…yes…oh, hi Peter…how are you? Yes, I can do that. Sure, I know how very important that account is. Great! See you then."

"Everything ok?" Drew asked.

"Yes. Just work." Cora answered. "I have to work late one day next week. We have a tough deadline. Now, where were we?"

Drew leaned over quickly and kissed Cora, wrapping his arms around her.

"Another Bourbon before I leave?" He asked Cora.

"Of course."

The goodnight kiss was long and embracing. Cora closed her eyes and melted into his arms. She wanted him to stay but she knew it was much too soon and he appeared to be too much of a gentleman to let that happen, at least for now. That night she made up day dreams about the two of them but pushed aside the thought that maybe he was a bit controlling.

Monday rolled around again and Cora prepared for a long night at work. After a hectic but successful day, Cora was happy for the invitation to dinner by her co-workers to celebrate. Sitting with her back to the door of the restaurant, she did not notice that Drew had walked in and positioned himself behind her. He put his hands on her eyes and said 'guess who'. Cora turned quickly to come face to face with him.

"Drew!" She shouted as she turned around and came face-to-face with him. "What are you doing here? How did you know where I was?"

"Well, I went to your office and the guard said that you and some other co-workers had gone to dinner." Drew said. "I figured you'd walked to the nearest restaurant, and here I am."

Cora was speechless. She could smell alcohol on his breath.

"Aren't you going to introduce us to your friend, Cora?" One of her co-workers asked.

"Yes, of course." She answered, trying to smile. "Drew Jackson, this is everyone; everyone, this is Drew Jackson."

"Have a seat." Someone said.

"Would you like something to eat?"

"Oh, no, thanks." Drew said. "But I would like a Bourbon and coke." He said as he pulled up a chair and sat down next to Cora.

Cora was so embarrassed that she became speechless throughout the remainder of the evening. When it was time to leave, she led the way out of the restaurant and after saying a quick goodnight to everyone, walked away toward her car with Drew following close behind.

"Hey!" He yelled out. Cora continued to walk toward her car when Drew yelled out again.

"Hey!" Drew yelled out a third time and began to run toward Cora, who began to walk faster. He grabbed her arm and jerked her toward him.

"I was talking to you and I know you heard me!" He said, gripping her arm tighter and tighter.

"Let go of me!" Cora yelled. "You're hurting me!"

Drew let go of Cora's arm and raised his hands in the air as if he was being arrested.

"Ok…ok…I was just trying to get your attention."

"You have a helluva way of getting my attention!" Cora said, angrily. "You hurt me!"

"I know, and I'm so very sorry. I didn't realize I was holding you so tightly. Please, I really didn't mean to hurt you!"

"Well you did!" Cora said, reaching her parked car. As she tried to get inside, Drew grabbed her arm again. Cora pulled away and slammed the car door shut. She hit the accelerator and drove away as fast as she could, leaving Drew standing in the street. As she sped away, she began to cry and cried all the way to her apartment. As soon as she opened the door to the apartment, she could hear the phone ringing. She knew who it was and she refused to answer.

- CHAPTER 4 -

THE ENGAGEMENT

As happy as Cora had been was as unhappy as she now was. It had been two weeks since the night Drew had grabbed her by the arm and even though he had gone far overboard, she still missed the attention, she missed him.

Early one weekday afternoon as Cora was talking to a client on the phone in her office, she was informed that she had a guest at the Information Desk. She quickly ended her call and headed toward the Information Desk where Drew was standing. He was holding a large bouquet of Red Roses in his hands and smiling broadly.

"What are you doing here?" She whispered so no one could hear her.

"I came to see you." He answered. "Here, these are for you." He said as he handed the Roses to her. "I'm sorry! I've been thinking about what I did and I just came to say I didn't realize how tight I was holding onto you. I just didn't want you to leave."

Cora glared at Drew. She was uncertain just how to respond...to simply walk away and keep her dignity, or to wrap her arms around him and tell him just how much she had missed him. Instead, she led him down the hallway to her office. Once inside, Drew pleaded his case to Cora.

"I swear it'll never happen again! Just give me another chance to show you how much I care about you. These past weeks have been miserable for me. I just can't get you out of my mind."

Cora put her head down. "I've missed you, too, Drew. But you not only hurt me, you scared me. I wasn't sure what you were going to do to me!"

There was an awkward silence again. Drew reached for Cora's hand and moved closer to her. She allowed him. He kissed her gently on the cheek.

"I promise you, Drew, if anything like that happens again you will never see me again…not ever…and I mean it!"

"Maybe we could have dinner this weekend." Drew said quietly.

"I'd like that." Cora answered, smiling.

Months went by. Drew and Cora spent as much time together as possible and every night on the telephone before each turned in for the night. Cora finally felt comfortable with Drew again and began to think seriously about introducing him to her father.

"How about a cookout?" Cora asked her sister Leslie. "We could invite Dad, Drew and his nephew, Darrell and whatever new sweetheart you have!"

"Sounds good to me." Leslie answered. "So, you're really going to introduce Drew to dad, huh? Must be serious."

Cora smiled but deep inside she was still skeptical of Drew. Was he a violent man that hid his temper and one day he would explode? Cora knew he liked to drink but she had yet to see him drunk. How far would he go with too many drinks inside of himself? She pushed the thoughts out of her head and continued to plan the cookout with Leslie.

"Hamburgers, hot dogs, plenty of sides and a nice green salad!" Cora said excitedly.

"Iced tea or lemonade?" Leslie asked. "Oh, and don't forget your boy's Bourbon!"

"I'm sure he'll bring his own." Cora replied.

The weekend of the cookout finally came. Everything was set up outside for grilling the food and enjoying the beautiful weather. It was obvious that Autumn was on its way and this would be one of the final summer weekends of the year. Leslie arrived first with their dad.

"Hi dad." Cora said. "Have a seat over here in this chair so you can watch the television, if you want to."

Just as she had situated her dad on the chair, the doorbell rang. It was Drew and his nephew, Darrell. Drew came in, just as Cora had said, with his own bottle of Bourbon and a six-pack of coke. He walked over and kissed Cora on the cheek and put the Bourbon and coke in the kitchen.

"Drew, this is our dad, Chester Dupuis. Dad, this is Drew Jackson." Cora said.

"Nice to meet you, Mr. Dupuis." Drew said, shaking Mr. Dupuis' hand. "It's a pleasure to finally meet you."

"You, too." Mr. Dupuis said. "And what did you say your name was again?"

"Drew, Drew Jackson."

"He did it again," Leslie said, leading Cora into the kitchen. "Did you hear how dad asked Drew what his name was immediately after you introduced the two of them. I tell you, Cora, it's early onset dementia!"

"I still don't believe that!" Cora whispered. "He's only sixty-five years old! He probably didn't hear me when I introduced the two of them."

"Believe what you want." Leslie said. "I know what I know and dad is just not acting right."

"Ok…ok!" We'll talk about it another time."

"Everything okay?" Drew asked as he poured himself a drink.

"Oh, yes." Cora answered. "Just putting Leslie in check!" Cora laughed.

The last person to arrive for the cookout was Jonathan Brown, Leslie's new friend. Cora was so very excited to meet him because Leslie had been through a bad breakup about a year before. She had not said a word about the breakup until Cora started seeing Drew.

"Nice to meet you, Jonathan." Everyone said. He found his way to Leslie and the two sat down on the couch next to Drew and Cora.

The cookout was a great success. Drew and Mr. Dupuis spent lots of time together discussing sports, soul music and, of course jazz. Cora was so happy to see the two getting along so well. She did, however, keep her eye on the number of drinks Drew was consuming while he chatted with her father. By the time all of the guests began to leave, Drew had consumed more than five glasses of Bourbon and coke. Cora was convinced that Drew could not drive himself home so she made a bed for him on the couch. He agreed that he needed to sleep before trying to go home and Cora hid his keys in her bedroom, closed the door and went to bed.

Cora was awakened the next morning by a soft knock on her bedroom door.

"Good morning, sunshine." Drew said as he slowly opened the bedroom door.

Cora stretched, smiling. "What's that scrumptious smell?" she said as she rolled out of bed, slipped into her robe and slippers and headed toward the kitchen.

"I forgot to tell you, I'm also a great cook. Coffee?"

"Absolutely!" Cora answered, seating herself at the kitchen table.

Drew prepared a breakfast plate of bacon, eggs and toast for the two and sat down next to Cora at the table.

"Hmmm. Delicious!" Cora said. "And you even knew how I like my eggs."

"So, what are we doing today?" Drew asked.

"Well, I've got laundry to do and an apartment to clean from yesterday's cookout."

"Oh," Drew said. "I also forgot to tell you I'm an excellent housekeeper."

Cora smiled.

"We'll get the cleaning out of the way, and then we can go shopping." Drew said matter-of-factly.

"Shopping? For what?" Cora asked.

"Your engagement ring, of course!"

Cora was shocked. "Engagement ring?" she asked.

"Yes, Cora Dupuis. I'm asking you to marry me!" Drew said, taking her hand. "I love you and I want to spend the rest of my life with you."

Cora was so surprised that she could barely speak.

"But…"

"I figured it would be better to let you pick out your own ring so I know it will be the perfect one for you." Drew said interrupting her. "I never dreamed I would ever fall in love again after Elaine died. But I have and I thank God that you came into my life…so, let's eat up, get this place in order and find that perfect ring for you."

Cora stood to sit on Drew's lap and wrapped her arms around his shoulders. "I love you, too, Drew Jackson. And yes, I will marry you!"

The two finished their breakfast in the midst of giggles and second cups of coffee. Cora finally announced that she was going to take a quick shower and begin the chores of the day.

"Can I come with you?" Drew asked, seductively.

Cora grabbed his hand and led him toward the shower.

The morning went by quickly. Cora did the laundry while Drew helped to clear the debris from the cookout.

"Let's go!" Drew said, taking Cora's hand into his own. "I'm anxious to see what ring you're going to choose."

It was another beautiful day as Drew drove the car toward the jewelry store. Cora's heart was beating so fast that she was afraid Drew could hear it through her chest. He put his hand on top of hers as they drove into the parking lot of the jewelry store.

"I want you to pick out exactly what you want!" Drew said as the two walked into the jewelry store.

"May I help you?" The clerk asked.

"Yes," Drew answered. "The lady is looking for her perfect engagement ring."

"Of course. Right over here." The clerk said, leading the way to the glass case that held engagement rings.

Cora took a deep breath and scanned the beautiful rings in the case with tear-filled eyes. It only took a matter of minutes for her to choose a simple oval shaped diamond ring.

"This one." She said smiling. "This is the perfect one for me."

"Wonderful choice." The clerk said as he took the ring from the case. He gave the ring to Drew who slipped it onto Cora's ring finger. Tears began to run down Cora's cheeks.

"It's a little loose." Cora said. "But it's the one I want."

"No problem." The clerk said. "We'll size it and have it ready for you this week."

Cora admired the ring on her finger as Drew filled out the paperwork. The clerk came back with the ring sizers and measured Cora's finger.

"Just come by Wednesday before closing. It should be ready by then."

"Thank you." Cora said, taking the ring off slowly and giving it to the clerk.

"You're sure this is the ring you want?" Drew asked. "I'm about to sign the invoice."

Cora laughed. "I'm absolutely sure!"

The drive back to Cora's apartment was as pleasant as it had been driving to the jewelry store. The two held hands while Cora put her head on Drew's shoulder.

Once back at Cora's apartment, Drew gave Cora a quick kiss and headed toward the door.

"Won't you stay for dinner?" Cora asked.

"I'll be back on Wednesday. We can have dinner then and I'll propose to you properly!"

He kissed Cora, grabbed the remaining Bourbon and coke and kissed Cora again just before closing the door to the apartment. Cora ran straight to the telephone and called her sister, Leslie.

"He asked me to marry him!"

"What?" Leslie asked. "What did you say?"

"I said yes." Cora answered. "We even picked out the ring. It'll be ready on Wednesday!"

"Oh! My goodness!" Leslie said excitedly. "Congratulations! I am so happy for you! But the question is…when are you going to tell dad?"

"Probably this weekend. I'll stop by his house. He seems to like Drew a lot so I'm sure he'll be happy for us."

"I'm just so happy for you!" Leslie said again.

"Me, too!" Cora said. "Me, too!"

Cora made a visit to her dad's that next weekend and gave him the news.

"Drew and I are getting married, dad." Cora said. "You like him don't you?"

"Who are you marrying?" He asked, confused.

"Drew, dad. Remember him at the cookout at my apartment last weekend?"

Cora spent her time trying to refresh her father's memory.

"Yes." He finally said. "Congratulations!"

Cora realized at that moment that her dad was truly suffering from dementia.

- CHAPTER 5 -

WEDDING BELLS

Drew made reservations for the same restaurant that he and Cora had gone to on their first date. He picked up the ring on his lunch hour and made his way back to work. Once back home after work, he called Cora.

"Pick you up at 6:30pm." Drew said to Cora. "Reservations are for 7pm."

"I'll be ready." She said. "I can't wait!"

Drew arrived at Cora's apartment at exactly 6:30pm. He knocked on the door and hid the bouquet of flowers behind his back. Cora opened the door and smiled when she saw Drew. He gave the flowers to Cora and kissed her.

"They're beautiful!" Cora said. "Let me put these in water and we can be on our way."

The drive to the restaurant was very pleasant. Great music filled the car from the radio while Drew and Cora held hands. Once at the restaurant, Cora squealed when she realized that they would be having dinner at the same restaurant they had had on their first date.

"I love this place!" Cora said.

"I'm so glad." Drew replied.

Once seated, Drew ordered his familiar Bourbon and coke for himself and a White Zinfandel for Cora. He seemed a little nervous.

"Are you okay?" Cora asked.

"Oh, yes. Of course. Just a little hungry. I didn't have lunch today, too busy."

It would be after dinner at a quiet table in the bar that Drew would give the ring to Cora.

"Cora Jackson, I love you! Will you marry me?" Drew said, slipping the ring on her finger.

"Oh! Yes, yes I will marry you!" She answered, with tears flowing down her cheeks. She leaned over the table and kissed Drew. "I love you, too, so very much!"

The two spent the night at Drew's apartment across town from the restaurant. It was an evening of conversation about their future.

"My parents passed on years ago." Drew said. "The irony was that my mom passed on first because of cancer; my dad died several years ago because of a heart attack and then my wife. I've lost everything I've ever loved."

"You won't lose me." Cora responded. "I'll always be here."

"It's time to pick out a house." Drew told Cora. "Something as perfect to you as your engagement ring."

"That sounds wonderful." Cora said. "I have a friend that's a Real Estate Agent. I'll call her this week. I'm sure she has some houses we can look at. What do you think?"

"Great!" Drew said. "At least three bedrooms. We have to have plenty of room for the children!"

"Wow!" Cora said. "How many children are we thinking?"

"Oh, just two or three. I'm an only child. I know what it's like to be growing up alone. All I had were my cousins that I spend summers with. I don't want our children to feel that loneliness."

Cora put her hand against Drew's cheek.

"Two or three it is!" She said.

Drew and Cora talked for hours while he drank several glasses of his Bourbon and coke. It was apparent that he was quite tipsy when Cora suggested they go to bed. By that time, she was beginning to believe that Drew definitely had a problem with alcohol, but she dismissed the thought while looking lovingly at her engagement ring.

Monday morning found Drew and Cora at their respective jobs. Cora was so thrilled to share her good news and her new engagement ring with her friends at work. There were 'oohs' and 'ahhs' throughout the day as friends and co-workers stopped by her office to offer their congratulations and see her ring. During the day, Cora made a call to her friend, Jenny, the Real Estate Agent that she had spoken to Drew about.

"I have several houses around the areas you're interested in. How about we make an appointment for Saturday to check them out."

"Super!" Cora said. "Just tell me where we should meet you."

Jenny gave her the address to the first house and set a time to meet.

"Sounds good." Drew said when Cora called him from her office. "I'm anxious to see the houses."

"Me, too!" Cora said. "Talk to you tonight."

Several of the ladies that worked in Cora's office planned an evening out to celebrate Cora's engagement. Dinner and drinks was the theme of the evening and Cora told Drew that night over the phone about the plan.

"We're just going down the street after work on Friday for dinner and drinks. I should be home around 10pm or so. I'll call you when I get home." Cora told Drew.

"Have a good time." Drew responded.

Drew got off early from work and drove to the building where Cora worked. He parked across the street and waited until he saw Cora and her friends walking to the restaurant. He got out of the car and began to watch them as they crossed the street to the restaurant. Peering in the window from a short distance, he saw them as they sat down at the table. Cora was laughing and enjoying herself. Drew entered the restaurant and sat at a distance from Cora's table at the bar where he could see her but she could not see him. He ordered his usual Bourbon and coke and stared at Cora and her friends until they began to leave. Paying his tab, he left the restaurant and walked toward his car before Cora and her friends left the restaurant. Driving away, he turned the music up loud in the car and banged on the steering wheel with his hands.

Cora raced into her apartment and ran to the telephone to call Drew. He answered, pretending to have been asleep.

"Did I wake you up?" Cora asked.

"No, I was just about to fall asleep."

"I'm so sorry." She said. "Go on to sleep. We'll talk in the morning."

"It's okay, baby." Drew said. "How was your night out with the girls?"

"Wonderful! But it was nothing like being with you." Cora said.

"That's good to hear." He said. "I love you."

"I love you, too, Drew. Goodnight."

The next day Drew and Cora met at the first house that Jenny had found for them to look at. The two agreed to look at all of the houses that the agent had for them to see and each would choose the one that was their favorite. Late in the day, the two sat outside of a café for coffee and to discuss which house each one had chosen. Surprisingly, both had chosen the same house! A split-level house with three bedrooms upstairs and a guest room downstairs with a family room and a fireplace.

"I can't believe we chose the same house!" Cora said.

"I can." Drew said. "Another reason to know that we are meant to be together."

It would be another month before the two could begin to move their belongings into the new house because of closing and other administrative paperwork. Both Drew and Cora took several vacation days from work to move into the new house. Plans were being made for a mid-January Wedding. Cora chose her sister, Leslie, as her Maid of Honor and Drew chose his nephew, Darrell as his Best Man. The two made all of the arrangements for the Wedding while downstairs in their new house laying by the fireplace.

Leslie planned a bachelorette party for the Friday night before the Sunday Wedding. It would be held at a local Tap House with a guest room for the girls to have their party. Drew told Cora to have a good time but was parked in the lot at her apartment when Leslie picked her up. He followed Leslie's car to the Tap House and parked far away from the building in the dark where he could not be seen. He could see the girls from the window but stayed inside his car this time, drinking his Bourbon and coke. As he did before, he waited until Cora and her friends began to wrap up the party to drive away.

It would be after midnight when Cora finally made it home after packing her car with all of the presents her friends had gotten her. She decided to leave them in the trunk of the car until the next morning and went to sleep. She knew Drew was probably asleep and waited until the next morning to call him.

"I had the best time and we have the best gifts ever!" Cora told Drew. "I wish you could have been there!"

The weather brought a chill in the evening air and announced that winter was on its way. With just a couple of months left before the

Wedding, Drew and Cora spent their evenings decorating the new house and putting the final touches on the day ahead.

It was a chilly day in January when Cora slipped into the Bride's Room of her Church. Leslie was with her and so were the three Bridesmaids. It was 1pm and the Wedding itself was scheduled for 2pm. Cora had had her hair and makeup done that morning and was now ready to put on her gown and have pictures taken.

"You look absolutely beautiful!" Leslie said to Cora after she put the veil on her head. The Photographer took pictures of her in her gown and before long it was time to take positions for the Wedding. Leslie sneaked a peek at the inside of the Sanctuary of the Church and squealed.

"This place is full of people!" Leslie said.

"Don't scare me like that!" Cora said. "I'm already shaking."

The music began and the bridesmaids took their places with the groomsmen to march into the Church sanctuary. Once they had made their way to the front of the Sanctuary, the Wedding March began and Cora, with her dad, began the walk down the white pathway to the front. She could see Drew. He was smiling and so was she.

"Who gives this woman to be married?" The Minister asked.

"I do." Chester Dupuis said and kissed Cora on the cheek.

Once Chester was seated, the Minister began the Wedding ceremony. At the end of the vows, he presented the bride and groom to the community.

"You may now kiss the bride! Brothers and sisters, I present Mr. and Mrs. Drew and Cora Jackson."

As the two kissed there was a roar of applause and plenty of tears to celebrate. Leslie hugged her sister with tears flowing from her eyes as Chester Dupuis hugged both of his daughters and shook Drew's hand. It was a wonderful Wedding.

During the wedding reception, which was held in the main hall of the Church, Drew and Cora danced together to the soulful sounds of "Tonight I Celebrate My Love for You" by Peabo Bryson and Roberta Flack. After the reception, Drew and Cora left for their seven-day honeymoon. Little did Cora know that she would conceive their first child during the luxury cruise ship headed for the Caribbean nation of St. Lucia's.

- CHAPTER 6 -

AND BABY MAKES THREE

Drew and Cora slipped back into the everyday grind of work after their beautiful Wedding and luxurious honeymoon. Shortly after returning home, Drew made a surprise visit to Cora's job. Noticing that she was not in her office, he dared to walk around the department and found her standing in the hallway talking to a man that he did not recognize.

"Drew!" Cora said, surprised. "Hi!"

"Hi." He answered. "Aren't you going to introduce me to your friend?"

"Oh, yes." She said, unsure. "Mr. Crenshaw, this is my husband, Drew. Honey, this is Mr. Crenshaw. He's here this week to audit…"

"Can I talk to you?" Drew interrupted.

"Why yes. Why don't you wait for me in my office?" Cora said, embarrassed. "I'll be there in a minute."

It was apparent to Cora and to Mr. Crenshaw that Drew was being aggressive and would probably embarrass her even more if she didn't take him to her office.

"Mr. Crenshaw." Cora said. "I'll be with you in just a few minutes, if that's okay with you."

"Of course." Mr. Crenshaw said. "We'll continue our discussion when you are free."

Cora led the way to her office. Once inside she closed the door and, with hands on her hips. began to tell Drew how important Mr. Crenshaw was to the company and that Drew could just not walk into her office anytime he wanted.

"Is that all that's important to you? Your job?" Drew said loudly.

"Not so loud, Drew, please." Cora said. There was a moment of silence as Drew stared at Cora angrily. Finally, Cora spoke out.

"Why are you here anyway?"

"There's talk that my position might be being transferred to Kentucky." He said.

"Kentucky!" Cora said, frowning.

"It's just a rumor for now but I wanted you to know as soon as possible so you could be prepared."

"Drew, we could have talked about this at home." Cora said, opening the door to her office. "I have got to get back to work."

Drew walked toward the door and as he began to walk into the hallway, he squeezed her arm so tightly that Cora leaned against the door and took a quick breath. She was so afraid that other people had seen Drew grab her arm.

"You're hurting me!" Cora whispered. He released the grip on her arm and kissed her softly on her forehead.

"I'll see you at home." Drew said. Cora cast her eyes down and slowly rubbed her arm.

"I love you."

Once Drew was gone, Cora breathed deeply and returned to the spot where she had left Mr. Crenshaw to finish their conversation. The afternoon lingered on but Cora was glad. She was not anxious to go home.

Cora opened the door to the house and was greeted by the aroma of dinner cooking and soft music playing.

"Hi honey." Drew said, taking her purse and her coat to put them on the couch. "How was the rest of your day?"

Cora stared at Drew.

"How do you think it was after your visit?" Cora asked.

"Baby, I was just so worried about my job and I didn't want the news to catch you off guard." Drew replied.

"You have a bad habit of grabbing my arm." Cora said as she passed by him to go into the kitchen.

"I know. I know. And I'm working on it." Drew said. "The last thing I want to do is hurt you. I love you so much!"

"But you do hurt me." Cora said, sitting down at the dining room table. She took her jacket off and showed Drew the bruise he had left on her arm. "You hurt me, whether you intend to or not."

"Look! I cooked dinner for us." Drew said, ignoring the bruise while lifting the top of the pot and blowing the steam toward Cora so she could smell what was cooking. "One of your favorites…Chicken Cacciatore with Spaghetti noodles!" He bent down to kiss her on the lips. Cora did not move but she could smell the Bourbon on his breath.

"Come on, baby! I'm just so nervous about the possibility of having to move to Kentucky, of all places." Drew said. "You know I didn't mean to hurt you. I'm so sorry!"

Cora could feel herself relaxing and giving in to Drew's antics. She felt that she understood his fears about the job and a possible move to Kentucky. She shook her head slowly and leaned up to kiss him.

"I'll never hurt you." Drew said calmly.

Cor discovered she was pregnant weeks later when she was sure she had missed her period and purchased a pregnancy test. The positive sign brought a smile and tears of joy to her and she was so anxious to tell Drew but in a special way. She stopped by a baby shop on her way home and scanned all of the many baby items for sale. Her eyes finally rested on a pair of baby booties. Scooping them up and holding them tightly as she walked up to the register, Cora decided that she would tie them around the rearview mirror of Drew's car while he was asleep. She giggled to herself as she drove home.

The evening went by as usual; dinner, a little television and bed. Once Drew began to snore softly, Cora sneaked out of bed and tied the baby booties to the rearview mirror and quietly went back to bed. The next morning Drew kissed Cora goodbye as she grabbed her coat and purse. She stood at the door as he began to back the car out of the driveway. He stopped suddenly, stepped out of the car and held up the baby booties. Cora shook her head 'yes' and smiled broadly. Drew ran to the door.

"Are you sure?"

"Yep." Cora answered, smiling. "The test was positive."

Drew hugged Cora tightly and whispered how happy he was.

"I'm so happy!" He said. "A little Drew, Jr."

"Or a little Cora, Jr." She answered.

The months went by as Cora went through the normal symptoms of early pregnancy; nausea, cramping and cravings. Drew was with her throughout all of the above and was at her side the day the ultrasound told her she was carrying a baby girl.

"Daddy's little girl!" Cora said as Drew smiled. "I like the name Nicole." He told Cora.

"I like Marie." She said. "Nicole Marie."

"Marie Nicole sounds better." Drew said.

Drew was at work when Cora's water broke. She had begun her maternity leave two weeks before her due date but Marie Nicole was coming early. She called him, called her sister, Leslie, and their dad just before she called the doctor. She grabbed her hospital bag with hers and the baby's clothes to come home and waited for Drew to drive up. He was as nervous as a cat as he helped Cora into the car.

"I'm sure we have lots of time." Cora said. "Just take your time."

The car sped through the neighborhood and down the freeway to the hospital where Cora was met by a nurse with a wheelchair. Drew followed the wheelchair to the labor hall and watched nervously as the nurse prepared Cora for the birth of their baby.

"Just relax." The nurse said. "It'll be awhile."

Hours went by and Cora finally began to labor intensively. What had been quiet conversation between Drew and Cora was now groans and moans as she labored closer to birth. Drew tried his best to help her breathe through the labor pains and push when it was time. Finally, in the early hours of the next day, Marie Nicole was born…Six pounds and eight ounces; 21 inches long with a head full of hair. It was obvious that the two could not love her more!

Marie Nicole was Baptized at two weeks old at the family Church. Drew and Cora agreed that Leslie would be the Godmother and Darrell would be the Godfather. A small reception was held at the Jackson house for family and friends immediately following the Baptism.

CHAPTER 7

CRASH AND BURN

The years went by quickly. Marie was growing straight and tall while the rumors continued about a possible move to Kentucky. Cora noticed that Drew was drinking more frequently and in greater quantities. She spent her time caring for the two of them and soothing herself about Drew's drinking with every excuse she could think of. She was content and in spite of the minor difficulties, life seemed to be going well for the Jackson family.

One Saturday evening, while eight-year-old Marie was spending time with her Godmother, Leslie, Drew asked Cora to fix him a Bourbon and coke as he laid on the couch. Even though she was hesitant, Cora fixed the drink and walked over to the couch to give it to him. Drops of water from the glass splashed on Drew and he slapped the glass out of Cora's hand. Sick of his drinking, she slapped him across the cheek without thinking. Drew got up from the couch as Cora began to run toward the bedroom. He reached inside the door and grabbed her before she could lock the door. Pushing her toward the wall, he banged her head against it and with his fist, hit her and knocked her out. When Cora finally woke up, Drew was lying on top of her trying to have sex with her. She realized where she was and what was happening when the phone began to ring.

"Get off me!" She yelled at Drew.

As she raised up from the bed, she felt the pain in her head and her eye where he had hit her. As she touched her head, blood was on her hand. She answered the phone as he sat on the side of the bed. It was Leslie.

"Just checking on you two." Leslie said. "Marie is getting a little anxious to go home."

"Oh! Yes. I'll be there shortly."

"I'll get her." Drew said.

"Are you scared my family will notice my eye or the blood on my head?" She said sarcastically. "Yes. You get her while I clean myself up."

"Cora…" Drew said, reaching for her. "I don't know what got into me! I'm so sorry, baby."

"I know what got into you." She replied. "Bourbon. Drew, you drink too much. I'll ask Leslie bring Marie home."

"What? You don't trust me to get my daughter?"

"OUR daughter, and no, I don't trust you. You're drunk!"

"I've been drinking but I'm not drunk!" Drew said as Cora went into the bathroom and slammed the door. "Open the door, Cora. I need to see what's wrong with your head."

"Leave me alone." Cora screamed through the door. After a few minutes she came out of the bathroom and reached for the telephone to call her sister.

"Leslie. Can you bring Marie home?" She asked when Leslie answered the telephone.

"Of course." Leslie answered. "Is everything okay?"

"Yes." Cora answered. "Everything is just fine."

"Great!" Leslie said. "I'll be there soon. I need to talk to you about dad. His symptoms are getting a little worse."

"I'll be here." Cora said. She went back into the bathroom and put makeup where her face and eye were already turning red.

"You know it was your fault." Drew said, standing in the bathroom door. "I wouldn't have reacted like that if you hadn't poured water on me and slapped me. You hit me first!"

Cora stood quietly in the bathroom. He was right; she had hit him first. What got into her? Was it her fault that the fight happened? She slowly walked past Drew to answer the door. It was Leslie with Marie.

"Hello." Leslie said as Marie ran in the door and straight into her father's arms.

"Come in, sis." Drew said. "Sit down and stay awhile."

Leslie sat down as Cora came out of the bathroom. She sat down next to her sister and hugged her daughter.

"I won't stay but a few minutes but I wanted to tell you that dad might not be able to stay by himself for too much longer. Sometimes when I call him, he doesn't recognize who I am. When was the last time you talked to him.?"

"Just a couple of days ago." Cora said. "But I didn't get that feeling. I mean I agree something's happening. Should we get an appointment with his doctor to have him checked out?"

"I'll call Doctor Lancaster this week and get an appointment, but we can't tell him what it's for. He'll never go, if we tell him it's to check for dementia."

"Let me know when the appointment is and I'll meet you there." Cora said slowly.

"Are you okay?" Leslie asked suspiciously. "What's wrong with your face? You look all puffy!"

"Oh!" Cora said. "I think I have a food allergy or something. I might have eaten shellfish or something accidentally. I don't know. It's not serious."

"Oh dear." Leslie said, concerned. "You look pretty bad. Are you sure you don't need to go to the doctor?"

"No." Cora answered sharply. "I have an Epi Pen if things get serious, but I don't think they will."

"You just make sure to call me if it gets serious! Gotta run. Love you all! Bye Marie!"

That night Cora slept clinging to the edge of her side of the bed. When Drew rolled over to touch her, she clung even closer to the edge.

"Not tonight." She told Drew. I have a headache."

Leslie called Chester Dupuis' doctor on Monday and explained the situation about her dad.

"It's noticeable enough to know something is definitely wrong with him but please don't tell him what you're looking for. He's very healthy otherwise and I think it would kill him to think we're looking for dementia."

"I understand." Dr. Lancaster said. "Bring him in on Thursday and I'll check him out."

"Thank you." Leslie said.

That evening she called Cora and they planned to meet at the doctor's office the next Thursday. Cora was able to take off a few hours from work to be with her dad for the examination. There was no apparent problem with Chester Dupuis recognizing his daughters that day but he could not fool the doctor.

"Your father is more than likely in the second stage of dementia; very mild decline. From what you have told me and my examination, I would say my findings are correct. It's hard to really tell at this stage."

"Oh no!" Leslie said, tearing up. "How long does he have before it gets worse?"

"That's really up to him." Doctor Lancaster said. "Right now it's minor memory loss; who someone is or where something is. It will slowly get more noticeable."

Cora grabbed Leslie's hand and began to cry.

"Can he live alone?" Cora asked.

"For now. Just be aware of the progression of the disease."

The two sisters held hands as they walked with their dad to their cars.

"See? There's nothing wrong with me but getting old!" Chester Dupuis said laughing.

"Yes, dad." They said as Chester Dupuis got into Leslie's car.

Cora could hardly concentrate on work when she returned to her office. Between being beaten up by Drew and the news about her father, her mind was torn in different directions. She was happy when five o'clock came and she could go home. But, she wasn't happy to go home, except for Marie. She was always happy to be with Marie.

- CHAPTER 8 -

KENTUCKY

What had been just a rumor for such a long time was now a reality; the Jacksons were being transferred to Lexington, Kentucky. Drew's new job would be at Lexmark in the Engineering Department. The three-month transfer period meant the family had to sell Cora's car and their house, relocate, find a new home, and enroll Marie in school all within ninety days. Cora was devastated. She could not imagine leaving her home, her sister and her father, her job…but she was even more uncertain about Drew who was still drinking. She was concerned about the next time he would raise his hand to her and she was concerned about being so far away from home if he did.

"Don't you see?" Drew asked. "It's a brand, new opportunity for us to start over, forget about the past. I told you I will never touch you again in anger."

"I've heard that before." Cora said, under her breath.

"At first I was scared about the move, but the money's right and I've heard the area is really nice." Drew said. "Come on, baby, be happy for me…for all of us!"

Cora walked away solemnly. Her mind was spinning around in circles as she hoped this was just a dream and soon, she would wake up. She realized that her place was with her husband but this home was all she had ever known.

"Hey, Cora!" Drew yelled from the bedroom as he surfed through the computer. "Look at these homes! They're just beautiful!"

Cora hesitantly went into the bedroom to join Drew. She sat down on the bed next to the computer. Drew was right; the homes were beautiful and the prices seemed to be in their price range.

"What about schools, Drew?" Cora asked.

"There seems to be a school in every district!" He answered excitedly. "I think we need to make a trip up there and see for ourselves. You should make application at the University of Kentucky and Toyota for jobs. With your experience, you should be a shoe-in anywhere you apply."

Cora agreed that a weekend trip would be the thing to do and the two began to make plans to drive to Lexington for a long weekend within the next two weeks. The idea was to contact Real Estate Agencies in areas close to Lexmark.

"I know you're not serious!" Leslie said when Cora spoke to her on the phone. "What about dad?"

"Oh, Leslie, this is hard enough on me. Don't put dad in the middle. I feel very guilty, but I'll do everything I can to help."

"Now how are you going to do that when you'll be almost a thousand miles away!" Leslie said, angrily.

"Maybe I could take him with me!" Cora said. "I could find the best doctors in Kentucky and just bring him with me."

"No." Leslie said matter-of-factly. "That is not an option. I take care of dad, always have. You took care of mom. "That's how it always was, and that's how it will remain. You can just stop by when you can."

Leslie hung up the phone and Cora began to cry.

Telling Marie was not quite as hard. She was going to miss her friends and her school but at her age, friends could be easy to make. Next, she knew she had to tell her boss and all of her friends at work. She knew she had to tell her boss as soon as possible so that he could find someone to take her place and so that she could train that person. Cora felt like her life was falling apart.

The drive from Texas to Kentucky was long and grueling. Even spending the night in a hotel halfway left over five-hundred miles to reach their destination. Both Drew and Cora complained to each other that they should have flown! During that weekend, Drew and Cora looked at several houses but both were drawn to a split-level house that reminded both of their house in Texas. It was just a couple of miles from Drew's job and on the school bus line to the school Marie would attend. There were plenty of shopping centers, restaurants and markets within driving and even walking distance. The area boasted tree-lined streets and shops within walking distance.

"It's not bad." Cora said, smiling.

"It's perfect! A new beginning." Drew answered, confidently.

Saying goodbye to her family and friends was the most difficult thing Cora had ever had to do. Of course, there were goodbye parties and gifts for the new house but none of that could make up for the heartbreak she was feeling.

"Oh, dad!" Cora said, kissing him on the cheek. "I'll be back soon."

"Don't...don't tell him that." Leslie whispered. "He's already having a tough time about you leaving."

The Jackson's hit the highway toward Kentucky before dawn with a full tank of gas and a cooler filled with snacks for Marie. Cora cried throughout the entire trip. Neither Drew nor Marie could offer her the comfort that she needed. Drew drove until dark the first day and pulled into a motel for the night. The family had Pizza for dinner, showered and then went to bed. Cora tossed and turned all night long and was wide awake when the alarm rang at 4:00a.m. Drew and Marie were excited to get back on the road, but Cora was fighting back tears.

'Welcome to Kentucky' the sign said as the Jacksons drove out of the state of Tennessee and into the Commonwealth of Kentucky. Drew and Marie clapped their hands.

"I'm glad you two are so excited!" Cora said sadly.

"I'm just happy to be here!" Drew said. "Just a couple of hours and we'll be out of the car. That in itself is enough to be happy about."

The Kentucky sky was blue, dotted with fluffy white clouds. Marie pointed out the different shapes to her dad and amused herself with singing to the music on the radio. The last two hours seemed the longest. Drew drove the car into the driveway of the hotel where he had made reservations for a time unknown once they reached Lexington. The furniture would not be delivered to the new house for another week so the family would be staying at the hotel at least until then. That, too, was reason enough for Cora to cry.

The day the furniture was to be delivered was the happiest day for Cora. She directed the movers where to place each piece of furniture and the boxes in the appropriate rooms. Marie was very happy with her room and enjoyed putting her things in just the right place. Cora spent that first day making beds and putting away dishes in the kitchen. It was beginning to feel a little bit like home.

"So, when are you going to start making application for jobs?" Drew said to Cora as they prepared for bed the first night in their new home.

"We haven't even finished unpacking yet!" Cora answered. "I think getting this place in order is the first priority."

"You do intend to get a job, don't you?" Drew said, raising his voice.

"Of course, I do, but we just got here. I didn't even have my work clothes until today." Cora answered. "Besides, what's the rush? We have money in the bank. Once I go to work, I won't have the time to fix up the house like I can right now."

"Yeah, well, I think you need to think about getting back to work. The money in the bank won't be there forever!"

Drew stared at Cora as though he was staring straight through her. She didn't answer anymore because she was afraid that he might hurt her. He had been drinking his celebratory Bourbon and coke, as he put it so Cora decided it was time for her to just go to sleep.

Several days later, Cora dropped Drew off and after she had enrolled Marie in her new school, she made her way to several businesses to make application and drop off her resume. She explained to each of the Human Resources Departments that she was just moving to Lexington and that her telephone would be hooked up within the week so she would check back as soon as it was. After picking Marie up from school, Cora changed clothes and headed out to pick up Drew.

"I went to a bunch of businesses today and left my resume. As soon as the phone is hooked up, I'll call each one to see if they want to interview me." Cora told Drew as she drove the family home.

"Now that's what I'm talking about!" Drew said. "Let's stop somewhere and get dinner. I'm sure you've had a busy day."

Cora was right. Several of the businesses where she had applied were interested in interviewing her. She scheduled the appointments and, one-by-one, she interviewed. She was offered three positions but was most interested in the Administrative Assistant position at the Lexington Herald-Leader newspaper. The current Administrative Assistant was leaving to have her baby but had decided not to come back to work. The job was available.

The building was located downtown Lexington with plenty of parking space and a nice financial offer. If the position was offered to her, she would work Monday through Friday from 9:00am to 5:00pm with an hour for lunch. With the interview at the newspaper company, Cora also had to take a typing test that she aced. Two days later, Human Resources at the Lexington Herald-Leader called to offer Cora the job. Drew was thrilled.

"We need to go shopping for another car this weekend." Drew said.

Cora agreed and found herself finally relaxing and becoming accustomed to the charm of the city of Lexington.

- CHAPTER 9 -

NEW BEGINNINGS

The first day of work at the Lexington Herald-Leader was exciting; meeting all of her fellow employees and learning about the business from classified and display advertising to printing and administrative duties. Ella Williams, the outgoing Administrative Assistant, was eager to show Cora everything she knew about the business and even invited her for lunch, a quaint little restaurant just across the street from the building.

"The newspaper," Ella said, "had its beginnings way back in 1870 and was known as the Lexington Daily Press. In 1895, it became known as the Morning Herald and later renamed the Lexington Herald. In 1888, a competitive afternoon newspaper named the Leader came into being and in 1937, the owner of the Leader purchased the Herald. The two operated independently of each other for 46 years but published a combined Sunday edition. In 1973, both the Herald and the Leader were purchased by Knight Newspapers. Knight merged and became known as Knight Ridder. A decade later, in 1983, the two newspapers merged and became known as the Lexington Herald-Leader."

"Wow!" Cora said. "Some history!"

"And that's just a succinct version!" Ella said, smiling. "But equally important is the men's basketball team here…the Kentucky Wildcats! The first season was in 1903. Lexington is definitely Wildcat country!"

Before Cora knew it, Ella was gone and the job was all hers! Although she had been well trained and knew the job, Cora still felt a little uncomfortable. But as time went on, she became the competent Administrative Assistant that she had been in Texas.

Home was another situation. Drew was drinking more and more, and had several times threatened to hurt Cora if she didn't do what he told her to do. He seemed to have two personalities; an angry man when he was drunk and the loving man she married when he was sober. She had often considered leaving but feared he'd track her down and escalate the violence. Besides, Marie loved her dad and he loved her.

The years went by quickly. Marie was almost fourteen-years-old. Cora was content but very cautious of her husband. He had pulled her hair, slapped her around and even threatened to kill her but Cora was faithful to him and continually made excuses at work for why her eye was black, or why there were bruises on her arms. She knew it would end one day, one way or another, so she began putting aside money in a separate bank account. But for now, she tried very hard to keep out of Drew's way as much as possible.

Drew came home from work in the best of moods one Friday evening.

"Let's grill out." He said smiling. "Take some steaks out and I'll fire up the grill."

"Sounds good to me." Cora replied. "I'm pretty tired.

The evening went by smoothly even though Drew was drinking heavily. Cora began to clean the kitchen after dinner and was at the sink when Drew pressed himself against her. He began to kiss her on her neck and put his hand under her skirt.

"Drew don't! Marie is in her room."

"Then let's go to bed, lock the door." Drew said as he continued to touch her.

"Don't!" Cora said, pulling away from Drew.

He continued to press against her.

"I said no, Drew!" Cora whispered.

Drew lifted his hand and backhanded her before she could react. She spun around and smacked her right hand on the handle of the microwave on top of the stove and screamed.

"Oh my God! I think you broke my hand!"

"It's your fault! I'm your husband." Drew said. "You have no right to deny me what I want, when I want it!"

"You're drunk!"

Cora began to cry and ran to the bedroom, slamming the door. Her face was red and her hand was throbbing. Marie came out of her bedroom.

"Daddy, what's going on?" She asked.

"It's okay, honey. Go back to your room." Drew told his daughter.

"Is mom alright?" Marie asked.

"I'm okay." Cora said, opening the door. "I slipped in the kitchen and hit my hand, Marie, but I'm okay."

Marie looked at her mom curiously. She was not so certain that was exactly what had happened.

"Let me see your hand." Drew demanded.

"I'm fine." Cora said, jerking her hand away from Drew. "Marie, I think I need to go to the emergency room. You stay here with your dad. I'll be back soon."

She grabbed her purse from the couch and began to walk to the door.

"Remember." Drew said. "It's your fault!"

Cora heard those words over and over again as she drove to the hospital. The pain was excruciating. Once inside, she registered at the front desk and explained to the clerk that she had fallen in the kitchen, hit her hand on something and thought she'd broken it. While waiting, Cora had plenty of time to think. Cora realized the situation was escalating and resolved to end the nightmare for Marie's sake and her own. Cora knew she had to have a plan, a way to get away from Drew. She planned at that moment to begin putting money aside to secretively find a place for her and Marie to escape.

After x-rays, the doctor told Cora that she had indeed broken a small bone in her hand and needed a cast. Cora put her head down. How was she going to be able to work with a cast? She thought some more as the cast was being put on her hand and made up her mind that this was the last time that Drew was going to hurt her.

When she finally returned home, Marie was asleep on the couch and Drew had sobered up.

"Baby, I'm sorry!" Drew said, trying to hug Cora. She pulled away and woke Marie up to send her to her bedroom.

"Mom, are you alright?" Marie said, sleepily.

"Of course, I am." Cora said smiling. "Go to bed now." She hugged Marie and went to her own bedroom followed by Drew. She sat down on the side of the bed.

"Drew, I want a divorce." Cora said, staring at the bedroom wall.

"A divorce?" Drew repeated.

"Yes! A divorce." Cora said, looking Drew straight in the eye. "I won't live like this anymore, wondering when you're going to hurt me again. You drink too much and I'm always the target of your rage."

"After all I've done for this family!" Drew said. He paused for a few moments. "You just need a good night's sleep. We'll talk about this in the morning.

Cora clutched the edge of the mattress, her knuckles white, and didn't sleep a wink.

"Can we talk?" Drew asked Cora as she slipped into her robe and slippers.

"We talked last night." Cora answered. "I want a divorce."

- CHAPTER 10 -

IRRECONCILABLE DIFFERENCES

Monday morning found Cora explaining to her boss and coworkers what had happened to her hand.

"I slipped on something on the floor and fell. I hit my face and my hand on something as I fell. Clumsy me! Silly, isn't it?"

Cora closed her office door at lunch and searched online for a divorce attorney. She found a divorce attorney just down the street from the newspaper office and made an appointment for the next afternoon right after work. She was trembling when she opened the door to the office. Everyone was very friendly and accommodating, an experienced staff that knew the trials of a divorce.

"Mrs. Jackson?" A voice said, bringing Cora back to the present. "I'm Attorney Elizabeth Carlson." She held out her hand to shake Cora's as she returned the handshake. "If you would, please follow me to my office."

Once in the office, Attorney Carlson smiled and told Cora to be seated. "So, you are looking to file for a divorce."

"Yes." Cora said nervously.

"How long have you been married?" The attorney asked.

"Almost...fifteen...years now." Cora stuttered. "My, times goes by so fast."

"Yes." The Attorney said. "It really does. First of all, let me ask you, does the cast on your arm speak to spousal abuse?"

"No." Cora answered. "Actually, I fell…" She paused and put her head down. "Yes. My husband hit me and I fell, hitting my hand and breaking it. I should be out of this cast in just a few weeks."

"Was this the first time?"

"No." Cora said hesitantly, putting her head down. "But I don't want to divorce him for that; I want it to be because we just don't get along anymore. I'm afraid he'll hurt me, or worse, if I tell anyone."

"I understand." The attorney said. "But you're going to need some help. I will give you the number to the local women's shelter if you need to run away. The shelter also provides counseling."

Cora looked up at the attorney and wondered to herself 'when did things get this bad?'

"Let's talk about your rights." The attorney continued. "Do you have any children?"

"Yes." Cora stated. "One daughter, Marie. She's almost fifteen now."

"Does your husband abuse her?"

"Oh, no!" Cora said, shaking her head. "They love each other and I try to keep my abuse a secret from her."

"I see." The attorney said.

The meeting lasted approximately one-hour. The attorney explained Cora her rights and the two sorted out and recorded what Cora wanted from the divorce.

"I know I want the furniture, my car and child support for Marie."

"Of course. All of that sounds fair."

"I know I have to have a plan to get out of the house before he finds out that I've filed for divorce." Cora said. "I'm putting money aside to get a place before he finds out."

"Here is the information you'll need for the women's shelter." The attorney said, giving Cora the address and phone number. "There is someone on call twenty-four hours a day. The only thing they ask is that you don't tell your husband or anyone where the shelter is located."

"I wouldn't do that." Cora said, taking the information from the attorney. "What's next?"

"Well, we'll get the Petition for Divorce written up and submit it to the Court. Your husband will also be served with this petition."

"Please don't serve him at work!" Cora pleaded. "I don't want to embarrass him."

"He will be served wherever it's convenient, I'm afraid." The attorney said. Once the petition has been filed in the court, it will be about sixty-to-ninety days before the divorce is final. Of course, that depends on the availability of judges who will need to sign the Decree of Dissolution. Of course, he can contest the petition, file for custody of your minor child, etc."

"I won't keep him from Marie. I agree to visitation rights but I want full custody."

Cora called her sister, Leslie, on her way home from the attorney's office. She finally told her everything.

"I knew something was wrong when I brought Marie home that night. You said you were having an allergic reaction to something…maybe shell fish. I've never known you to be allergic to any foods but your face was all swollen and you were sweating. That bastard! You and Marie come back home! Dad and I need you here." Leslie said.

"I'm not leaving another home." Cora said. "Marie is just going to have to know the truth."

When Cora arrived at the house, dinner was cooked and Drew was playing a video game with Marie. Both were excited to see her.

"Why so late?" Drew asked.

"I had a meeting."

"No, you didn't!" Drew said. "I called your office."

"I was at another office." Cora said.

"Okay, okay." Drew said sarcastically.

Cora just picked at her dinner and soon after announced that she was going to bed. What had become the normal, she gripped the side of the mattress and then tossed and turned all night while the odor of liquor filled the room. The next morning Cora prepared for work without saying anything to Drew even though he attempted several times to talk to her.

"Have a great day, Marie." Cora said. "I love you very much!"

At work again, Cora called the 24-hour service at the women's shelter. She was adamant about moving out of the house before Drew found out she had filed for divorce.

Not knowing exactly when the petition would be served to Drew, Cora began to pack their clothes and hid the suitcases at the top of Marie's closet in her room. She knew that she and Marie would have to be out of the house, somewhere Drew would not think to look as soon as possible. She knew the abuse would be much worse than it already had been if she was still in the house when Drew was served the petition.

"Marie, your dad and I love you very much." Cora explained to Marie. "But he has a drinking problem, and when he drinks, he gets angry…at me."

"I already know, mom." Marie interrupted. "I hear you crying sometime, and I know you didn't slip in the kitchen and break your hand. You either have a black eye or bruises on your arms all the time. I know he hurts you, mom, and if this is the way to make it stop, then this is the best thing."

Cora hugged Marie. "I didn't want to have to tell you all of this, I'm so sorry. Your dad is going to be served divorce papers soon and he is not going to be very happy about that. You and I need to get out of the house and hide somewhere he won't know where we are. Do you understand this?"

Marie shook her head 'yes' and began to cry. "When are we leaving?" She asked.

"As soon as I can find a place for us to live that won't be obvious to your dad."

And with that, Cora began to search for another house that would meet their needs. She made up her mind to take the first house that she visited but, during a lunch hour, a real estate agent showed her a three-bedroom house located at Alabaster Court, on the same bus line with Marie's school. The house was for rent, not for sale, but that was okay with Cora. Marie was now in high school, planning out her own life including attending college at Eastern Kentucky University, just up the road from Lexington. And besides, Cora was only looking for a temporary place for her and Marie to feel safe.

The owner, now living in Florida, had returned to show Cora the house. He spent lots of time with Cora, telling her how his daughter was found dead in the swimming pool in the back year. It was apparent that he was still grieving and wanted someone that would preserve the memory and take good care of the house.

"I'll take it!" Cora said. "When can we move in? It's pretty important that my daughter and I move in as soon as possible. I'll pay whatever you want."

Mr. Davis could see that Cora was anxious about something. He told her how much the deposit and monthly rent would be. Cora took out her checkbook, wrote the check and gave it to Mr. Davis.

"I have a blank lease in my car. I do require a one-year lease." He said.

"Oh! That's fine." Cora answered. She quickly signed the lease and shook Mr. Davis' hand.

"I can't thank you enough!" Cora said. "We really need a place to stay, and right now."

Mr. Davis gave Cora the keys to the house and gave her his address in Florida. He returned to his car and told Cora goodbye as he drove away from Alabaster Court.

Cora took a Personal Day from work the next day but dressed as if she was going to work so that Drew would have no idea what she was up to. She said goodbye to him and drove toward her job until Drew turned to go toward his job. She quickly returned to the house, grabbed the suitcases from Marie's closet and drove to the house in Alabaster Court. Putting the suitcases in the house, she went to a nearby department store and bought sleeping bags. She picked Marie up from school and the two went to the rental house, closed and locked the door. The next day, Cora told her boss and a friend in building security that she had filed for divorce and that her husband might try to get to her in some way once he was served the petition. She also called Marie's school and told them not to sign out Marie to anyone but herself.

When Drew was served, he called Cora at work and showed up at Marie's school, just as she'd feared. Neither place accommodated him. He even tried to pick Marie up from the parents' line but Cora was able to get her first, and as Drew was following her, Cora led him to the police department. The two would not see each other again until they were face-to-face in divorce court. Cora agreed that Drew could spend time with Marie every other weekend and some holidays at a place they agreed upon. Drew tried several times to talk to Cora but she refused to talk to him. Eventually, Drew would leave Cora alone and concentrate on his relationship with Marie.

- CHAPTER 11 -

SAFE AT LAST

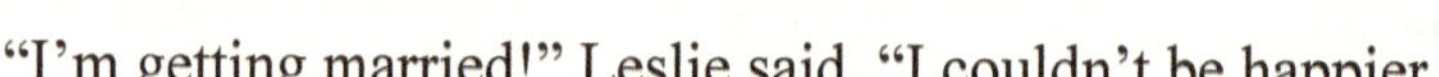

"I'm getting married!" Leslie said. "I couldn't be happier.

"And I couldn't be happier for you little sis!" Cora said excitedly.

"Of course, you'll be my Maid of Honor!" Leslie continued. Both girls screamed.

"And what about dad?" Cora asked. "How is he?"

"Not so good." Leslie answered. "Somedays he has full clarity and some days he doesn't even know who I am. The doctors say he's at Stage 5, moderately severe cognitive decline. It's very difficult."

"I'd like to bring dad here, to Kentucky, with me." Cora said sincerely. "I need to do this. The University of Kentucky Medical Center has some of the finest doctors in the country. Besides, you need a life now with your husband. Give me some nieces and nephews to love on."

"You don't need to do that! Calvin and I can handle it."

"Yeah, well, so can Marie and I handle it."

After the wedding, Chester packed his bags, ready to go. He was lightly sedated for the flight to Kentucky to keep him, as well as Cora and Marie, comfortable. Once they were home, Cora settled her dad in the spare room and called her sister to let her know that all was well.

Within the next year, Drew announced to Marie that his job was being transferred back to Texas. Marie was devastated but Drew promised see her often, and that she could come to Texas as often as she wanted. It would be at that point in time that Cora and Marie began to be at odds with one another.

One particular weekend night, Marie asked Cora to go to a party with some college students. Cora said 'no' and the two began to argue. Marie was sent to her room.

"I'm eighteen-years-old, mom! You can't keep me in the house forever." Marie said.

"Well, as long as you live in my house…"

The next morning, when Cora checked on Marie, she was gone. Detective Carl Spencer from Missing Persons arrived to investigate. The next day, he located Marie at a friend's house and escorted her home. Detective Spenser visited with Marie quite often and became a good friend to the family.

"Hi, Detective Spenser." Cora said as she opened the door to her house on a Saturday afternoon.

"After all this time you should be comfortable enough to call me Carl."

"Okay…Carl. Marie is not here today. She's in Texas with her dad. I'll tell her you stopped by. She'll be disappointed." Cora answered.

"Thank you." Carl said. "But I'm not here to see Marie today." He smiled. I'm here to see you!" Cora smiled back and slowly opened the door.

Book III

The McKenzie's

- CHAPTER 1 -

DJ AND LORI ANN

David John McKenzie, nicknamed "DJ" as he was growing up, was born and raised in Bowling Green, in the western portion of the Commonwealth of Kentucky. His father was a pharmacist who worked at a large national chain department store and his mother was a piano teacher at the local music store, and also offered lessons in her home. The two had three children; David, the oldest, Adam and Patricia. DJ's parents always thought he had the makings of a great lawyer. He often argued in defense of his younger siblings when they were caught misbehaving. And, as fate would have it, DJ did grow up to be a great Defense Attorney.

Having hardly ever left the confines of Bowling Green as he was growing up, DJ viewed Lexington as the place to attend college, the "big city" and he was mesmerized by the University of Kentucky when he visited with his parents in his senior year. He wrote the letter required for the application packet with all the eagerness of a young lawyer.

Northeast of Bowling Green, in the small town of Lima, Ohio, lived a young girl named Lori Ann Carter, the youngest of three girls; Patty, Missy and Lori. Her mother called her "little Lori" while her father called her "princess". Little Lori may have been a princess to her dad but to herself, being a nurse was what the future was calling her to be. She played nurse with her dolls, with her sisters and with her mother when time permitted. Lori's father owned an automotive shop and often came home with cuts and scrapes on his hands, the perfect situation for an up-and- coming nurse! Lori's mother, on the other hand, was a stay-at-home mom that raised the girls and that kept the books for the family business.

When it was time for Lori to choose the school of higher learning she would attend, she made the choice to the attend the University of Kentucky as well because of the highly recognized School of Nursing. During her senior year, Lori and her parents made the journey to Lexington and spent the day preparing to say "yes" to the invitation for her to attend.

That summer, just prior to leaving for UK, DJ McKenzie and Lori Carter spent their time packing, saying their goodbyes to friends and daydreaming about being a Kentucky Wildcat! Their parents, however, spent their time already missing their children and planning when they would be coming back home for a visit. The freshmen were driven to their dorms by their parents who found themselves crying as they said their goodbyes.

"I'm proud of you, son." Mr. McKenzie said to DJ. "Do your best!"

"I will, dad." DJ responded. "That's all I've got is my best!"

The two hugged good bye as Mrs. McKenzie reached to hug her son. Tears flowed down her cheeks as she gripped him tightly.

"Don't cry, maw." DJ said. "I'll be home before you know it! Just be sure to send me some care packages."

"Of course." Mrs. McKenzie said. "Care packages every week!"

Across the large University campus, the same scene was being played out with the Carter family. Little Lori found herself crying as she hugged her father goodbye. It was her mother, however, that stressed the importance of school work as opposed to partying.

I know!" Lori snapped. "That's why I'm here, to learn."

"Now, now." Mr. Carter said. "Do your work and then you can party!"

He winked at his daughter and hugged her one more time before the two parents disappeared from the dorm room. Lori smiled but deep inside she knew that she would miss her parents and the security of home.

It was apparent that her new roommate had already chosen her side of the room because there were suitcases on the bed and clothes hanging in the closet. Lori wondered to herself where she was at the moment and how well they would get along.

Just a few moments after DJ's parents left his dorm room, a very buff young man knocked on the door.

"Hi." The young man said. "I think I'm your roommate!"

DJ smiled and shook the young man's hand.

"I hope you don't mind that I took this side of the room." DJ said.

"Oh, no problem." He answered. "After all, you were here first. My name is Robert Jordan but everybody I know calls me Buddy."

"Well, Buddy, I'm David McKenzie but everybody calls me DJ!"

The two laughed and began to set-up their new home.

"What's your major?" DJ asked Buddy.

"Physical Education." He answered. "My goal is to be a Coach. What's yours?

"Oh, Law. I've always wanted to be a Lawyer, ever since I can remember."

"Me, too." Buddy said. "I've always wanted to be a Coach."

"You certainly look like one already!" DJ said smiling.

"Wrestling!" Buddy said excitedly. "Been wrestling ever since I was in middle school."

"Wow!" DJ said. "I've played a little football but I'm really not very athletic."

"That's alright," Buddy said. "I won't hold that against you!"

Across campus, Lori was setting up her side of the room when her new roommate came in.

"Oh, you're here!" The young woman said with a sharp southern accent. "I was wondering when you would get here. My name is Kristen, Kristen Burdette from Memphis, Tennessee."

"Hi, Kristen." Lori said, extending her hand to greet her. I'm Lori Ann Carter from Lima, Ohio. So nice to meet you!"

"You, too!" Kristen said. "I got in this morning so I didn't think you'd mind what side of the room I took…"

"Oh, not at all." Lori said. "Either side is fine with me."

The two young women chatted about their goals for the future while putting their things away and settling in. Kristen shared that she was undecided exactly what she wanted to pursue at the moment but toyed between teaching something and business. Lori was very happy to tell Kristen that she was pursuing nursing.

"I'd thought about nursing once upon a time but realized early on that I couldn't stand the sight of blood! That did it for nursing!" Kristen said, laughing.

By the time darkness fell, both DJ and Lori, and their roommates had eaten dinner and found themselves preparing for bed. The next day would be filled with the excitement of the first day of college classes, finding the buildings in which they would be taught and becoming accustomed to running to and from the dorms in between.

Morning came quickly and even though DJ didn't have a class until later in the morning, Buddy was already up and exercising!

"Did I wake you?" Buddy asked apologetically.

"Naw." DJ answered. "I'm still on High School time."

"When's your first class?" Buddy asked.

"Not until 9:15." DJ answered. "I think I'll check out the cafeteria to see what they have for breakfast. When's your first class?"

"8:30." Buddy answered. "English…not my favorite class!"

Lori and Kristen were both awake at the break of dawn, excited and ready for class.

"My first class is across the campus." Lori said. "Psychology at 9:15. Think I'll walk over to the cafeteria for breakfast. Wanna come?"

"Sure!" Kristen answered. "My first class isn't until 11:00."

The cafeteria was busy with incoming freshmen and young people of all levels thereafter. DJ found himself in a line for freshly prepared eggs, standing in front of Lori and Kristen who had the same breakfast thought. When it was finally DJ's turn to order, Lori spoke out at the same time.

"Oh! I'm terribly sorry!" She said when she realized that she had cut in front of the young man.

"No problem." DJ said. "Go ahead. I'll order after you."

Lori was so embarrassed but that embarrassment would only be heightened when she saw DJ descending the stairs in her Psychology class. Their eyes met, and Lori scooted down in her chair as he sat himself in the seat next to her.

"Not only did you cut ahead of me at breakfast, now you've taken my seat!"

Lori gasped and began to stand up as DJ whispered "I'm just kidding! This is our first day in class. No one has a particular seat yet."

The two smiled at each other as DJ extended his hand to her.

"I'm DJ McKenzie."

"I'm Lori Carter. Very nice to meet you."

CHAPTER 2

WE'RE NOT IN HIGH SCHOOL ANYMORE!

Early to bed and early to rise was now the rule. Classes much of the day and homework assignments throughout much of the night kept DJ and Lori quite busy. But there was plenty of time for them to unconsciously look for each other in the cafeteria, the Psychology class and the student union where they had accidentally run into each other on several occasions.

Lori had little experience with boys in middle and high school, but she recognized her feelings and she was quite aware that she was beginning to have feelings for DJ. He, too, was beginning to think about her and promised himself that he would ask her for her phone number the very next time he saw her which would definitely be the next Psychology class. Lori, in turn, was wondering how she would respond if DJ would ever want to get to know her better. When the time was appropriate, DJ slipped his phone number in Lori's hand at the end of a class and told her to call him so they could chat and get to know each other. After all, the two were always running into each other…that had to mean something.

Since Lori and DJ would see each other regularly during the once per week class, Lori had some time to consider calling DJ. One evening, several days later while brushing her wet hair after a shower, Lori took DJ's phone number off of the bulletin board in front of her desk and punched in his phone number on her phone. It began to ring. Lori's heart was thumping loudly by the time DJ answered the phone.

"I was wondering if you were ever going to call me." DJ said before she could say hello.

"Now how did you know it was me?" Lori asked.

"Well, let's just say that I was hoping it was you!"

"Well." Lori said. "You were right, it's me."

The two talked for more than an hour that first night. Lori gave her phone number to DJ and told him that it would be his turn to call the next time they talked.

"You got a boyfriend already?" Kristen asked when Lori finally hung up the phone.

"No." Lori answered. "He's just a new friend.

"Sounds like more than just a new friend to me!" Kristen said smiling.

Lori returned the smile. "I think I would like him to be more but right now I've got school to think about. I did enjoy talking with him. Now that he has my phone number, I hope he'll return the call."

And that he did. In fact, DJ called Lori every single evening and both smiled broadly at each other when face-to-face in their Psychology class.

"What are you doing for lunch?" DJ asked Lori as they walked out of class.

"I hadn't really thought about it. Any ideas?" Lori asked.

"Maybe we could grab something and just sit outside." DJ suggested.

"Sounds good to me." Lori said.

The two walked to the cafeteria and grabbed "to go" boxes and found a spot outside to eat.

"When's you next class?" DJ asked Lori.

"Not until 2:00. When's your next class?"

"Actually, I'm done for the day. That's why I felt it was okay to ask you to have lunch with me." DJ answered.

"Well, I'm glad you did." Lori said.

"Yeah?"

"Yeah."

It would not be too long before DJ and Lori became a couple on campus, holding hands walking to class and long walks on the weekend at the Arboretum. During Thanksgiving break, when each went to their respective homes, they called each other several times per day and talked several hours before saying goodnight. At the end of that second semester, it was very obvious to both DJ and Lori that they were indeed in love. By that following spring, the two were talking about plans for a wedding.

During summer break before their third semester, Lori was in Lima, Ohio, and DJ was in Bowling Green, Kentucky but their plans were to meet each other's parents sometime before returning to school. Lori convinced her parents to stay in Lexington for a couple of days after bringing her back to school to meet DJ and his parents while DJ finally persuaded his parents to do the same. Both the McKenzie's and the Carter's were fully aware that there was something going on between their children but only after being asked to meet each other did they understand the seriousness of relationship.

Needless to say, it was a bit awkward at that first meeting. DJ made reservations at a local restaurant in downtown Lexington and hotel reservations at a downtown hotel for the night for the two families. The parents, along with their child, met at 6:30pm for dinner. The introductions were made with ease but the conversation between Mr. McKenzie and Mr. Carter eventually turned toward football, college football, dominating the entire first meeting. It was obvious that they liked each other but the conversation about DJ and Lori took second place to the Western Kentucky Hilltoppers and the Ohio Bobcats! The two women smiled at each other a lot and tried to strike up a conversation about the children to no avail but promised to stay in touch. At the end of the evening, the parents said goodnight and made plans for an early morning breakfast before each began heading back to their homes. DJ and Lori chose to have a goodnight drink before turning in.

"Do you think our dads gave a single thought to why we were altogether tonight?" Lori asked.

"Probably not." DJ answered. "But at least we introduced them to each other."

DJ asked Lori to marry him at Christmas of their third year at the University of Kentucky. The two chose to spend the Holiday at Lori's house in Lima where her mother had made up the guest room for DJ. His parents were very happy for the two of them although they missed having DJ home for Christmas. He had chosen the ring, with the help of his mother, during one of his free times while Lori was in class. DJ's mom suggested that he put the ring, in its small box, in much larger containers to trick her. Well, it worked! Lori opened the larger boxes one-a-time and laughed when she finally found the ring box.

"Lori, I love you." DJ said, taking the ring from her and slipping it on her ring finger. "I would have asked you to marry me the very first time I met you if I thought you would have said 'yes'. I hope you'll say yes now because I can't think of a future without you. Will you marry me?"

"Yes…yes, I will marry you!" Lori said, with tears falling from her eyes down her cheeks.

The two young people made a plan that night to wait until each had graduated college, prior to DJ attending Law School, before attempting to get married. Both agreed that Lexington would be the perfect place for them to live and raise their children because it was halfway between Bowling Green and Lima. Certainly, Lori would be able to find a job at a local hospital, after all the city was full of hospitals. There were also plenty of law firms in the city of Lexington and in the surrounding towns. At any rate, they would be together, working it all out together.

CHAPTER 3

MEET THE MCKENZIE'S

"Well, of course I'll be your best man!" Buddy said, patting DJ on the back. "I'm excited!"

"I'd like my little brother, Adam, to stand with you, if you don't mind. He's a little young to be planning a bachelor's party but I'd like him to be involved a little bit anyway."

"That sounds great!" Buddy said, patting DJ on the back again. DJ smiled.

"There's a lot to being a best man." DJ said. "You have to keep up with the ring as well as the bachelor's party."

"No problem." Buddy said.

Across campus Lori was calling her two sisters to ask one of them to be her maid of honor.

"You two decide when one is going to be the maid of honor and the other one can be a bridesmaid."

"You're the oldest, Patty." Missy said. "I'll help with the planning of the bachelorette party and all of the other things that need to be done but you stand next to Lori at the wedding."

"Are you sure, Missy?" Patty said.

"Of course, I am." Missy said.

"Well, that's that." Lori said.

"Where are you getting married?" Patty asked.

"We're not sure yet." Lori answered. "We thought about just getting married at the Chapel at the University and have the reception at one of the wineries…maybe. It would be unfair to our parents if we chose one city over the other, and besides, we are going to be living here after we're married."

"Sounded like it worked out alright." Kristen said.

"I guess so." Lori replied. "I just didn't want to hurt either one of their feelings. But I guess it is only right for Patty to be my maid of honor since she is the oldest."

"Well, of course!"

"Besides, they agreed to work together to get everything done so I guess they're all right with their decision." Lori answered. "Oh, and by the way. I wanted to ask you to be one of my bridesmaids."

"Me?" Kristen asked.

"Yes, you!" Lori answered. "We've been living together for almost four- years now so it's just inevitable that you are with me on my wedding day."

"Well, I humbly accept!" Kristen said, bowing with her hand over her heart.

The year flew by as DJ and Lori planned their graduations as well as their wedding. DJ had accepted a job as a Law Clerk in a downtown firm that he hoped would hire him once he graduated Law School and passed the Bar Exam. Lori began pursuing her Nursing career by accepting a part-time job at the University of Kentucky Medical Center to help ends meet as she also continued her nursing education.

Graduation came first and gave the opportunity for the parents along with DJ and Lori to make more wedding plans while together in

Lexington. The two found a small apartment close to the University where DJ would attend Law School with plans to move in after the wedding which was just weeks away. When the big day finally came, DJ and Lori tied the knot in front of family and friends in the University Chapel with the Reception held at the Talon Wineries. A honeymoon would follow in the future when the time was right, but for now, it was an exciting day.

Time was passing by quickly for the newlyweds. The three-years of Law School had passed and DJ was looking toward taking the Bar Exam. He had been hired by the Law Firm where he had been working as a Law Clerk while Lori had finished her Master's in Nursing and working full-time at the University Medical Center. All seemed to be progressing along as they had planned.

"Lori's voice trembled with excitement. 'I'm pregnant!

"Oh! My goodness!" DJ responded, catching his breath. "Great news!"

"Well, there goes our honeymoon." Lori said.

"No big deal." DJ said. "We can plan a weekend or two away before the baby comes."

The next person DJ told about the baby was his best friend, Buddy.

"Hey." DJ said excitedly. "We're pregnant!"

"Well, how about that!" Buddy answered. "So, what are you hoping for? A boy or girl? My Godchild, right?"

"I would have to say a boy but I'll take either, as long as it's healthy, as they say. And of course, we wouldn't have anyone else as a Godfather!"

Time was flying by and before long the McKenzie's had grown out of their apartment and looking for another one to accommodate their growing family. The two found and agreed upon a three-bedroom rental in one of the suburban areas of Lexington. DJ and Lori eagerly decorated the nursery and waited for the anticipated birth of their child.

Alexander John McKenzie was born a couple of weeks early weighing 7 lbs. and 12 oz., 19 ½ inches long; both mother and baby were doing well. Kathleen Anne McKenzie would be born two-years after her brother, weighing 6 lbs. and 8 oz., 21 ½ inches long. And just as promised, Buddy became Godfather to the first born. To DJ and Lori, their little family was complete.

Life was indeed good for the McKenzie family; DJ was now a full-fledged Attorney at the firm of his choice while Lori was now a Registered Nurse at one of the local hospitals. The children were growing quickly and before long, Alex was in Kindergarten and Katie was in pre-school. "Uncle Buddy", as Alex called him, was now a middle school Coach and was always around to give Alex the best clues on how to hold a baseball bat just right on a tee-ball stand or helping him to learn to swim. By the time Alex graduated from elementary school, he was an excellent baseball player and had joined the swim team. He did quite well in school and could beat anyone at electronic games.

Katie liked to follow her brother all over the place and especially enjoyed going to his baseball games or swim meets. When she was old enough, DJ and Lori bought Katie a trampoline that took up most of her time and freed her big brother of her 'company'.

It was now time to fulfill the McKenzie's plan of buying a house. Securing a Real Estate Agent, DJ and Lori visited several homes around the city of Lexington but to no avail; one was too small, one didn't have enough bathrooms while another was far out of the school district for the children. But just when the two were about ready to give up, another house…the perfect house popped up for sale.

"It's a split level with three bedrooms upstairs with a guest bedroom in the basement with a den; two-and-one-half baths…11732 Alabaster Court." The Agent said, describing the house. "It has a large fenced in yard as well. The neighborhood was built in the 1970's and most of the residents have been there for many years and not expected to move anytime soon. Would you like to look at it?"

"Sure!"

The Agent met the McKenzie's at the house. It only took fifteen-minutes for them to make up their minds.

"We'll take it!" DJ said.

The McKenzie family moved into the house on Alabaster Court during the summer. DJ made sure he had situated Katie's trampoline in just the right place in the backyard and she jumped high on it while the family moved in. Alex claimed his bedroom and began connecting his games; by the time everything was in place, the family was exhausted.

When it was time to register the children for school, Alex was extremely excited to know that he would be going to the middle school where his Uncle Buddy coached. Buddy showed DJ and Lori around the school and familiarized Alex with the athletic program. There was no swimming program but DJ promised he would find a swim program somewhere in the city.

Katie's school was right next door to Alex's school which made it easy to keep up with the school bus schedule. Alex would meet Katie and together they would catch the bus home from Katie's school.

One particular weekend, Alex heard noise coming from outside of the back of the house. Curious, he went to the back deck and looked toward the noise. It was coming from the house next door. Alex leaned over the rail and saw a group of teens in swimsuits splashing in the Davises' pool. Alex realized that they were older than him but he was enjoying the view. Shortly after discovering the young people, he went to the front of the court where he began to play basketball by himself. Suddenly, a beautiful young woman accompanied by a young man came out of the front door of the house where the party was being held. She was dressed in a skimpy bathing suit and he was wearing athletic shorts and a raggedy white tee shirt. Alex kept playing basketball but turned his attention away from the two when they began to kiss. The young man jumped in the car. The sound of the car was very loud, as if the muffler had fallen. As he backed his car out of the court, Alex just continued to play basketball.

"Hi there!" The sound of a woman's voice filled the air. Alex dropped the basketball and stared in the young woman's eyes. She extended her hand to his.

"I'm Charlotte Davis." She said. "You're the new kid, from the new family. What's your name?"

"Alex." He said quietly, after a couple moments of silence. "Alex McKenzie".

"Well, nice to meet you, Alex McKenzie. How do you like living here?"

"It's alright." Alex said.

"You don't talk much, do you?" She said, smiling.

"No." Alex answered. "I guess not."

"Well, welcome to the neighborhood!" Charlotte said. "Gotta' get back to my friends. Wanna' come and join us?"

"Oh, no, thank you." Alex said, knowing his mother would kill him if she knew he was hanging out with much older people.

"If you change your mind, you're always welcome." Charlotte said.

"Thank you."

Charlotte smiled and walked away towards her house. Alex found himself staring at her but quickly bowed his head and headed toward the basketball goal when she turned around to look at him. This would be the first time that Alex would talk to Charlotte Davis.

- Chapter 4 -

About Charlotte

I t didn't take very long for the McKenzie's to fit into the close-knit residents of Alabaster Court. They quickly fell into the routine of leaving food out for the neighborhood cat that had made its home in the Court long before the McKenzie's. Katie gladly took on that responsibility and never neglected her duties. Lori found herself having coffee with her neighbor, Pat Davis and having long conversations with Pat's best friend, Betty Eliason while they all stood at the mailbox.

Pat enjoyed talking about her daughter, Charlotte, a college student studying to be a Social Worker. Pat took the opportunity at Lori's first encounter with her to apologize for the summertime antics at the Davis's pool.

"She loves her friends!" Pat said. "And we love having them here so if the noise gets too loud, just let me know and I'll calm them down. Everyone can tell when her boyfriend, Brad, arrives with that loud muffler of his. We've even offered to get it fixed for him but he says it's his greeting to the neighbors…just saying hello."

DJ had developed a friendship with Pat's husband, Joe Davis. The two talked about cars, college basketball and drank beer on one or the other's porch. It was quite apparent to DJ that Joe was not very fond of Charlotte's boyfriend, Brad. He absolutely hated the sound of his car, the way he dressed and hoped she was not thinking of a serious relationship with him.

"I love my daughter and I don't mind the swim parties during the summer when she's home, but I just can't see her with this guy!"

"Well, so far Alex is more interested in his games than he is in girls…at least I think so. He's very quiet and spends a lot of time in his room. I'm sure the time will come soon!"

Alex found himself standing on the back deck, peering at the Davis' house when Charlotte was at home with her friends. He wished he could join their party but he knew his parents would never allow him to party with college kids. Alex spent much of his time playing basketball when Charlotte was at home and many times she would follow her boyfriend to his car and then talked to him when her boyfriend left.

"You sure like to play basketball, don't you?" Charlotte asked him one day. "Do you play at school?"

"Nah." Alex answered. "Baseball and swimming."

"What do you think about when you're playing basketball out here?"

"Oh, all sort of things." Alex answered. "I really like to play my games." He added, quickly changing the subject.

"Oh! Me, too!" Charlotte answered excitedly. "I'm pretty good, too!"

"For a girl…" Alex teased.

"What's your favorite game?" Charlotte asked.

"I guess I like them all." Alex answered.

The two laughed and Charlotte said her goodbyes, reminding Alex that he was always welcome to come to the pool parties when she was at home. Alex shook his head to thank her.

Katie smirked. "You like her! as Alex went back into the house. "I know you like her!"

Alex rolled his eyes. "You're crazy" and escaped into his room to play his games.

"No, I'm not!" Katie retorted. "I see you standing on the back deck watching her. You're the one that's crazy; crazy about Charlotte!"

Time passed by and life went on as usual. Charlotte went back to school and the swim parties were on hold until the next time. Alex secluded himself in his room playing his games while Katie jumped on her trampoline until the weather changed, bringing cold air and eventually snow.

The holidays came and the sound of Charlotte's boyfriend's car told Alex that she was at home. It was too cold for basketball so he knew he would not get to see her until the summertime parties.

"Alex, come her please." Lori's voice rang out through the house. "You have a package here."

"A package?" Alex asked as he ran towards his mother. "Who's it from?"

"I don't know." Lori answered. "It doesn't have a name or a postmark."

Alex quickly opened the package. It was a game with a note.

'Dear Alex. This is my favorite game. Perhaps we can play together sometime. Your friend…Charlotte. P.S. Be sure to practice. I'm pretty good, even for a girl!'

It was a video Soccer game. Alex smiled and ran upstairs clutching the game.

"Alex! It's almost dinner time." Lori yelled out. "Don't get too comfortable up there!" She quickly turned toward DJ. "Have you noticed how very quiet Alex has been lately?"

"All these teenagers are like that. They'd rather play those games than eat." DJ said. "It's better than him running the streets."

"I guess you're right." Lori said. "I guess I'm just worried for nothing."

2003 came in with a bang, a loud bang from the house next door where the students lived. The owner had hired a construction crew to make major repairs on the house, both inside and out, and the sound of hammers, drills and saws could be heard well into the night.

The summer of 2003 also brought Charlotte Davis back home from school and found Alex peering at her and her friends from the back deck. At one time, he was sure that she was peering back at him so he quickly ran back into the house. Despite being 'found out', Alex continued to sneak peeks and enjoy those moments of Charlotte's company whenever he could while he was playing basketball.

It would be on one of those warm summer nights that the residents of Alabaster Court would awaken to the sounds of sirens and lights, bright lights everywhere. Alex was already awake, playing the game that Charlotte had given to him when the police car, firetruck, ambulance and coroner turned down Alabaster Drive. He heard the sirens and for several minutes thought they would drive on by the Court, but instead, whatever tragedy there was had come to one of their homes.

DJ and Lori were awakened abruptly with the lights shining directly into their bedroom.

"Oh my God!" Lori yelled as she jumped out of bed and headed toward the children's bedrooms. DJ darted toward the stairs leading to the downstairs, grabbing his robe along the way. Both thought that there was a fire somewhere in the Court.

"Alex!" She said, opening the door to his room. "Are you all right?"

"I'm fine." He said, trembling.

Lori grabbed his hand and ran next door to Katie's room where she was putting on her robe.

"I'm okay, mom." She said.

The three ran down the stairs where DJ was standing on the front porch.

"It's not a fire but whatever it is, it's happening next door at the Davis' house. I could hear Pat screaming. I saw Betty just run across the Court to Pat's house as I was coming outside."

Other neighbors were now standing on their front porches wondering the same thing going through DJ's and Lori's mind…who could it be?

What seemed to be more than an hour passed when a body was moved on a gurney wrapped in black covering from the Davis' house. Lori scooted her children back into the house where they both peered out of Alex's bedroom window.

"What do you think happened?" Katie asked.

"I don't know…" Alex answered somberly. "But whatever it is, it's got to be really bad."

Betty Eliason was standing with Pat and Joe Davis in front of the house as the gurney was put into the ambulance. DJ caught Betty's eyes and she shook her head to let him know that whatever was happening at the Davis' house was truly a tragedy. It suddenly occurred to DJ and Lori that the body on the gurney was more than likely Charlotte Davis.

The sun rose over the Court. All of the neighbors, including the McKenzie's had gone inside of their homes. Alex lay awake, replaying the night's events. He knew in his heart that it was his friend, Charlotte and that whatever happened to her was for forever. He stared out of his bedroom window and began to cry.

CHAPTER 5

ABOUT BUDDY

Charlotte Davis's death sent shockwaves through Alabaster Court, with rumors spreading quickly. DJ and Lori told Alex and Katie that Charlotte had probably drowned in the backyard pool.

"But she was an excellent swimmer." Alex said. "She wouldn't have drowned in her pool."

"Well, there are lots of rumors, son." DJ said. "We'll have to wait until the detectives investigate everything. And when they do, we'll know the truth. In the meantime, don't listen to anything unless you hear it from me or your mother."

The McKenzies didn't attend Charlotte Davis's funeral because they thought it would be too much for Alex. As time went by, Alex began to withdraw more and more, spending most of his time playing games and skipping meals. DJ thought perhaps he was grieving the death of his friend but Lori was convinced it had to be more than that. Although his grades were consistent, Alex seemed to be distant and very rarely had conversations with the family.

"Maybe we should take him to some sort of Counselor." Lori told DJ. "He is so not like himself."

"Let's just give him some time. I'm sure he'll snap out of it." DJ replied.

But Alex did not 'snap out of it' and became more and more reclusive. He was showing very little interest in baseball when it was time for the season. He had even asked to skip swimming for the year. DJ agreed Alex might need a break.

"This is David McKenzie. May I help you?

"Hey DJ. It's Buddy." The voice on the other end of the phone whispered. "Busy?"

"Not much." DJ responded. "What's up?"

"Well, I've got a problem and believe it or not, I need you as an Attorney and a friend."

"Ok." DJ said. "So, what's going on with you?"

"I really don't want to talk about it on the phone." Buddy said. "Could you get away sometime soon for dinner?"

"Yes. Anything for you." DJ said, surfing through his appointment book. "How about Thursday night?"

"That sounds perfect." Buddy said.

"Hey, Buddy. You sound bad. Are you in some sort of trouble?" DJ asked.

"I sure hope not!" Buddy said. "See you Thursday. I'll send you a message about where to meet."

"Ok."

The two hung up the phone. DJ was very concerned about his best friend. What kind of trouble could he be in? Just what was he going to hear when he met with Buddy on Thursday? DJ was puzzled and found it hard to concentrate on his work at the Law Firm for the next few days. He also found it hard to sleep; Buddy kept coming to his mind.

Thursday finally came around. DJ closed out his day and made plans to meet Buddy when the phone rang.

"DJ, it's Buddy. I can't meet you for dinner."

DJ stood up from his desk and began to pace his office floor.

"Buddy, tell me what's going on."

"I'm in jail, DJ, and I need an Attorney right now."

"What?" DJ yelled, flopping down in his chair. "What the hell???"

"Can you represent me? I really need an Attorney and I would prefer it was you."

"Yeah, sure." DJ answered. "I'm on my way now."

All sorts of things went through DJ's mind as he drove across town to the jail. Buddy was sitting in the cell when DJ walked up to him.

"DJ." Buddy said, as a guard opened the cell for DJ to walk in.

"Are you going to tell me now what's going on?"

Buddy lowered his head.

"I've been accused of molesting some boys at the middle school."

DJ could not believe what he was hearing that he almost laughed.

"You've got to be joking!" DJ said.

"Nah, man." Buddy said. "This is for real and I'm scared to death."

"Well, how did this happen?"

"Some kid accused me and then two more stepped up. I've lost my job, DJ. I'll probably never be able to work in Lexington again."

"Calm down, Buddy." DJ said, trying to comfort him. "I have to ask you this…did you do this?"

"Of course not!" Buddy yelled, standing up and beginning to pace around the cell.

"Ok, Ok! I had to ask you!" DJ said.

"Do you believe me?" Buddy asked.

"Of course, I do." DJ responded.

"Then you'll represent me, right?"

"Yes, of course I'll represent you." DJ answered. "First, we need to get you out of here. I'll be back."

The guard opened the cell door and let DJ out.

"Don't worry!" DJ said. "We'll get through this together!"

DJ scanned through the prosecution's case against Buddy after he paid the bail for his charges and Buddy was released from jail.

"You're facing some heavy-duty charges, Buddy." DJ said as he and Buddy sat in the kitchen drinking coffee at the McKenzie's house early one morning. "Can you remember anything that you said or did that would cause these boys to accuse you of such things?"

"Nothing, DJ." Buddy said. "I treat all of the kids the same, like my own kids. I didn't do anything wrong."

DJ and Buddy were still sitting in the kitchen when Alex came downstairs for cereal and milk. His eyes bulged as he saw Buddy sitting in his kitchen.

"Hey, Godson!" Buddy said, reaching out to Alex for a hug. "Come and give me a hug. Haven't seen you in a while."

Alex backed out of the kitchen and bolted upstairs.

"Hey, Alex? What's up?" Buddy said.

"He's still grieving for his friend, Charlotte Davis, that passed away recently. We have to give him some space." DJ said.

Late that night, DJ found himself tossing and turning in his bed. He finally rolled out of bed and made his way downstairs for a glass of water. His mind was full of thoughts about his best friend. Suddenly, it came to

DJ that perhaps Alex knew something about the boys that were accusing Buddy of molesting them. Could that be why Alex was so standoffish from the man he had run toward since he was a toddler? He decided he would talk to Alex the next day.

The next day, DJ gathered his courage and slowly walked up the stairs to Alex's bedroom.

"Knock, Knock." He said. "Can I come in?"

"Yep." Alex said, playing his game.

"Can we put the game down for just a few minutes?" DJ asked. "There's something I'd like to talk to you about."

Alex sat up straight in his bed and put the game controllers down.

"Your Uncle Buddy has been accused of some pretty terrible things and has asked me to represent him. I was wondering if you knew or had heard anything about the boys who are accusing him?

"No." Alex said, quickly. "I don't know anything."

"Then why were you so cold, actually disrespectful to him yesterday?"

"Dad," Alex said. "I'm a little too old to play 'Uncle'. Besides, he's not really my Uncle, he's just your best friend."

"Ok." DJ said. "Fair enough."

"Can I finish my game now?" Alex asked?

"Sure." DJ said, as he turned to walk out of the door.

"Dad!" Alex called out to his dad.

"Yes, son."

After a short pause, Alex replied.

"Would you please close my door?"

"Of course." DJ closed the door and made his way back downstairs where Lori was sitting in the kitchen.

"Did you talk to him?" She asked.

"I did, but he said he didn't know anything about anything." DJ answered.

"To be honest with you, I don't believe him. He said he was too old to play

'Uncle' anymore, and that Buddy wasn't his real Uncle anyway."

"What do you think's gotten into him?" Lori asked.

"I don't know." DJ said. "But I think it's time we find out."

DJ walked toward the stairs and proceeded up to Alex's room, followed closely by a very concerned Lori. He knocked on the door and when DJ did not hear anything from Alex, he slowly opened the door to find him sitting on his bed with tears streaming down his cheeks.

"Alex!" Lori cried out, wrapping him up in her arms. "What's wrong? Why are you crying?"

"I think I know." Katie said, standing in the doorway.

"What do you know?" DJ asked.

"I think you both already know." Katie answered.

There was a long-time silence in the room while DJ tried to dismiss in his head and in his heart what he knew to be the truth, that Alex was actually one of Buddy's victims. He felt rage deep inside but walked over to his son and assured him that he would take care of the situation.

"I just don't want you to represent him!" Alex said, still crying.

"You can rest assured that I won't be representing him, son. Nor will any other defense attorney."

Lori held Alex tightly, realizing herself what had happened to her son.

"What are you going to do, DJ?" Lori asked.

"Like I said, I'm going to take care of the situation."

- CHAPTER 6 -

RESTITUTION

D J sped through the city of Lexington heading for Buddy's apartment. His jaws were clenched and his hands gripped the steering wheel tightly as the car went faster and faster, as if it had a mind all its own. DJ had called Buddy to make sure he would be at home when he arrived there, not letting on why he would be on his way.

"You son of a bitch!" DJ yelled as he burst through the door when Buddy opened it. DJ grabbed Buddy by the neck and began to hit him with his fists until he fell to the floor.

"You molested my son!" DJ said, still beating Buddy with his fists until his blood began to flow onto the carpeting. Buddy never said a word nor did he try to defend himself.

"You molested all of those boys! I could kill you…"

"DJ!" A woman's voice yelled out. "Stop DJ…you're going to kill him!"

It was Lori. She had followed DJ knowing where he was going and what he was going to do. Grabbing DJ, trying to pull him off of Buddy, Lori yelled out…

"He's not worth you going to prison, DJ! Please let go of him!"

DJ finally gained control of himself and looked at Lori.

"He touched our son!"

"Let's call the police, right now, and let the law handle it!" Lori said, holding onto DJ.

Buddy laid motionless on the floor. Lori dialed 911 and asked that police be sent to Buddy's apartment as soon as possible. DJ sat on the couch, putting his head in his hands.

"The police are on their way." Lori said, taking a seat on the couch next to him.

"Where's Alex?" DJ suddenly asked.

"He's with Katie, he's fine." Lori answered.

"How could we have not known about Buddy?" DJ asked somberly. "All of these years…"

"I know." Lori said, putting her arms around DJ's shoulders. "He fooled us all. He's been your best friend since college and never gave us a hint that he was a child molester."

"Now what?" DJ asked, looking toward Lori. "What happens to Alex? What about all of those other boys?"

Moments later, the sound of police sirens filled the air. By this time, Buddy remained on the floor, his head propped against a chair leg. Blood was flowing from his mouth.

"Attorney McKenzie!" A policeman who knew DJ from the court system said as he walked into the house. "What happened here?"

DJ explained the entire situation while the policeman took the report.

"Did you do all of this?" He asked DJ.

"I know I did but I can't even remember. I was so out of it!" DJ answered.

"You know I have to ask him if he wants to press charges against you." The policeman said.

Buddy's whisper was barely audible. 'No charges."

"Well, I doubt any court of law will prosecute you anyway, not after what you just told me."

The policeman began to put handcuffs on Buddy and jerked him to standing up. Buddy was still quiet but tears were streaming down his face.

"I'm so sorry, DJ!" Buddy said through his tears. "I just can't help…"

"Go to hell!" DJ yelled out. "I hope you burn in hell! And you can rest assured that I won't be representing you, nor will any other reputable attorney. I'll make sure of that. And as for me, I'll be too busy representing Alex and the other boys whose lives you've ruined!"

The policeman dragged Buddy to the car and after putting him into the back seat, drove off toward the station house.

"Are you okay to drive?" Lori asked DJ.

"Yeah, sure." DJ answered. I feel much better!"

Buddy was given a twenty-five-year maximum sentence for Child Molestation as well as Child Endangerment, with no chance of probation for his crimes against the children. Alex went to trade school to become a house painter and subsequently opened his own shop. The first house he painted was the home of Charlotte Davis.

BOOK IV

JoAnna and Melissa

- CHAPTER 1 -

FAREWELL

"Hi, mom." JoAnna O'Neill said as she answered the phone. "How are you?"

"Well, I have some news, bad news." Her mom said and then paused.

"What's up, Mom?" JoAnna asked concerned.

"Two things." She said. "Charlotte Davis was found dead in her parents' pool over the weekend."

"What?" JoAnna said, shocked. "What happened?"

"All I know so far is what I'm hearing. You know, rumors. I've heard that she drowned but then I heard someone actually murdered her."

"Oh, my goodness!" JoAnna said, finding herself pacing the floor in her office. "When's the funeral?"

"Sometime this weekend. The Davis' house and pool are now a crime scene so they have to wait for the investigation."

"I can't believe this! I just saw her during the holidays."

"I know." JoAnna's mother said. "So very sad."

"So, what else? What more bad news?"

"The biopsy came back today. I have stage four breast cancer."

"Oh, no, mom! That's the last thing I know you needed to hear." JoAnna said, somberly.

"Yes, it is," she replied

"So, what are the doctors saying? Will you have to have a mastectomy?"

"Yes, more than likely a double mastectomy, in the next couple of weeks. I have an appointment scheduled for next Tuesday and I'll know everything then."

"I'll be there, mom!" JoAnna said. "Please, don't worry."

Immediately after hanging the phone up, JoAnna went to the school's office where she worked.

"I need to take a few weeks off, beginning next week." She told the principle. "My mother is facing serious surgery and I need to be with her."

"I'm so very sorry." The principle said. "Yes, of course. Just keep me aware of how long you'll be out. And JoAnna, my best to your mother."

The next phone call she made was to Liz, her girlfriend of five years.

"Hey." She said when Liz answered the phone. "Got some bad news this morning. Mom's biopsy came back positive for stage four breast cancer."

"Oh, my goodness!" Liz said. "I know you're going to Kentucky. When are you leaving?"

"Next Monday. Her appointment is next Tuesday and I want to be there with her through all of it." JoAnna began to cry.

"I certainly understand that." Liz said. "If there's anything I can do to help, please let me know."

"I know, and I love you for that." JoAnna said. "I'm going to check on the flights for Monday and I'll be home."

"Ok." Liz said. "See you at home." The two hung up the phone.

JoAnna booked a 6:00 a.m. flight from Raleigh to Lexington, with a layover in Chicago. Once in Lexington, JoAnna rented a car and drove to her mother's house. She felt anxious about seeing her mother as she drove around New Circle Road. She had just been home about three-months before, during the holidays. Her mom had found the lump in her breast about two months after JoAnna's visit and shortly after that she would have the biopsy and now the news was that it was cancer.

JoAnna's mother was standing in the doorway when she drove into the driveway. She quickly jumped out of the car and after hugging her mother began to cry.

"Don't cry." Her mom said. "I'm not scared. Besides, it's been an awful long time since I've seen your dad." She began to laugh.

"Not funny." JoAnna said, wiping her eyes.

Sometime during the evening, JoAnna made her way to the Davis' house to pay her respects.

"I just can't believe she's gone!" JoAnna said to Joe and Pat Davis. "I was saying to myself that I had just seen her during the holidays. I'm so very sorry."

"Thank you for coming by." Pat Davis said. "She always enjoyed being with you and Meghan."

A double mastectomy would be performed on JoAnna's mom within two weeks of her coming home to Lexington. The doctor said that the cancer had spread throughout her body and gave her four-to-six months to live. JoAnna was devastated. She called her principle that day and resigned, explaining that her mother had been given a short time to live and that she needed to be with her as much as possible.

"Of course." The principle answered. "My deepest sympathy. If you ever find yourself in Raleigh again, call me. You were a great asset to the school and the students."

That night, JoAnna called Liz and explained the situation to her.

"I won't be home anytime soon. I've got to stay with my mother. I hope you understand."

Liz was silent for a few moments and then replied.

"How long will that be?"

"I don't know." JoAnna answered. "Longer than the school would probably hold my job, so I resigned."

"You did what?" Liz screamed over the phone. "You've just severed all of your connections to Raleigh!"

"So, that means you as well?" JoAnna asked.

"I didn't say that." Liz responded. "Let's not make this a bigger deal than it is right now. Do what you have to do."

JoAnna was with her mother every step of the way; from the surgery, through chemotherapy, and finally to her passing one solemn evening in the hospital. JoAnna had slipped out of her mother's room to take a short walk around the hospital floor, as was suggested by one of the Nurses. When she returned, minutes later, her mother had passed peacefully in her sleep. JoAnna's life was shattered.

In accordance with her mother's wishes, JoAnna had her mother cremated and spread her ashes in the backyard of her beloved home on Alabaster Court, around a tree in the Daffodils. It was that moment that JoAnna would make up her mind to stay in the house that her mother had left her and not return to North Carolina. She knew she had to tell Liz and she hoped that Liz would accept her suggestion that she quit her job and come to Kentucky to be with her. Unfortunately, Liz refused to leave her job and her home so both agreed that there was nothing keeping them together now. Their final goodbye was the finale to months of sadness, but JoAnna felt that she had made the right decision to stay in Lexington.

Alone in the house of her youth, JoAnna found it difficult to sleep. She thought of herself and Charlotte Davis as younger girls spending time together at her mother's house. She remembered how very happy they all with no thought of what she had just experienced.

"I need a job!" JoAnna thought out loud. "I need something to occupy my mind."

JoAnna scanned the listing of job openings for the coming school year from Human Resources on the Fayette County School's website. There were several listings but one caught her eye; a teaching position at a middle school not very far from her house on Alabaster Court. She felt herself getting very excited about the possibility. After filling out the application online, she went to the mailbox to retrieve the mail. Outside of advertisements and magazines, there was a booklet with a brand new schedule of Shows planned for the Singletary Center at the University of Kentucky. Once inside the house, she scanned through the booklet and made plans to purchase a ticket for the very next performance. Her mother and father had introduced her to Broadway Shows as well as the Opera as she was growing up and this would be just what she needed to finally settle into her new life.

JoAnna would soon receive a letter from Fayette County Schools to give her the date for her first interview with the middle school where she was hoping to teach. Everyone seemed to be impressed with her credentials and offered her the position. Life was beginning to look up.

- CHAPTER 2 -

MELISSA EDWARDS

The end of the summer had come to Kentucky and school was finally open. Students were practicing for football and other games that would be played during the Autumn season. JoAnna was as happy as she could be now, considering all the hurt she had had to experience. She loved teaching and she loved her students, even when she found herself having to discipline one or two of them.

JoAnna reminded herself in her boredom one Saturday afternoon that she had planned to attend a Show at the Singletary Center. She quickly found the booklet and saw that a Ballet was scheduled for that very evening. She changed clothes and was out the door in a matter of minutes. Once inside the Singletary Center, she walked quickly to the ticket window where there was a long line. By the time she made it to the window, the tickets had been sold out for the evening performance.

"I'm so sorry!" The young redhaired girl said. "I can offer you a 'rain check' for another performance.

"That would be great." JoAnna said. "When is the next performance?"

"The Matinee, tomorrow…2pm." She said, writing up the 'rain check' and handing it to JoAnna.

"Thank you so much." JoAnna said, smiling.

"You need to be here by 1:30pm to get your ticket at the 'Will Call' window."

"Thank you again. See you tomorrow." JoAnna said.

"Enjoy the show!" The young girl smiled and greeted the next customer.

The next day came quickly and JoAnna looked forward to going back to the Singletary Center for the Ballet. She prepared a quick lunch and found herself at the 'Will Call' window for her ticket. After getting her ticket, she passed by the ticket window and saw the young redhaired girl. She slipped quickly in front of the next person in line and said…

"Excuse me. Just wanted to say thank you for setting this up for me. Thank you again."

The girl smiled again and continued to take care of her other customers.

JoAnna found herself at the Singletary Center at least once per month, whether she liked the performance or not. She wasn't quite sure if her connection to the Singletary Center was for the performances, although they were excellent, or if she was attracted to the pretty, redheaded girl. She made up her mind that next time she was there she would ask her for her name.

"Hey." JoAnna said. "My name is JoAnna O'Neill. What a pleasure to meet you!"

She extended her hand out to shake hers. The girl took the cue and extended her hand and introduced herself.

"My name is Melissa, Melissa Edwards." She said with the smile that JoAnna had come to like. "Glad to know you're enjoying the performances here at the Singletary Center." She continued.

"I am, I really am." JoAnna replied.

She turned to see how many people were in the line behind her waiting to get tickets. JoAnna wasn't quite sure if Melissa would find it appropriate for her to invite her out for coffee but before she could stop herself, she had asked her the question.

"Coffee sometime?"

Melissa stopped smiling and paused to look at JoAnna.

"I get off early on weekends."

JoAnna quickly proceeded to get back into the ticket line. Once facing Melissa again at the window, she began to smile.

"I'd like a ticket for this Sunday's matinee."

Melissa smiled as well as she printed out the ticket.

"I hope you'll enjoy the performance."

"I'm sure I will." JoAnna replied.

The week went by slowly, each day filled with at high percent chance for rain. The days were dreary and the nights were warm. JoAnna concentrated her thoughts on school but occasionally the thoughts about Melissa creeped into her mind. She regretted not asking for her phone number. The two could be having interesting conversations while getting to know each other, especially on dreary, rainy days. Phone conversations might have been easier to discuss certain conversations than in person, but JoAnna had missed her opportunity to get her number but promised herself that she would get it on Sunday.

Sunday finally came. The threat for rain was there and JoAnna considered that while she tried to pick out that appropriate outfit.

"Should I dress like a teacher, or should I dress casually? Rain boots or loafers; khakis or jeans?' She thought as she scanned through her closet. She finally settled for a pair of khakis with a light, knit sweater and loafers. She twirled a lovely silk scarf around her neck and grabbed for her purse as she ran for the door. The closer she found herself getting to the Singletary Center the more anxious she became. She knew that she had to sit through the two-hour performance before she could be alone with Melissa so she took several deep breaths and entered the Center. She saw Melissa was busy tending to her customers. JoAnna slipped past her and entered the auditorium where the Performance would be held, found her seat and made herself comfortable in the chair. When the lights were dimmed on the stage, JoAnna became ready to be entertained. Once the Performance was over, JoAnna decided to wait until the rest of the people made their way to the Lobby and Melissa time to finish up her day's work. When JoAnna finally did make it to the Lobby, Melissa was standing in front of the ticket window with purse and sweater in hand.

"Hi there!" JoAnna said. "Good to see you."

"Oh, hi!" Melissa said, surprised. "I thought maybe I have missed you."

"No. I was waiting for everyone else to leave. I thought you might have some things to finish up so I took my time. So sorry if I made you wait. It's been a long time since I've been in Lexington so I'll have to rely on you to come up with a good coffee shop."

"No problem." Melissa said as the two left the Singletary Center. "There's a little shop not far from here, but we probably should drive since it just might rain."

"Good idea." JoAnna agreed.

"Well, I'm parked right over here." She said, pointing to a car parked right in front of the Center. I know I'm closer than you are."

The two entered the car and drove to the little Coffee Shop just a little ways from the Center and were able to get a table close to the door.

"This is nice." JoAnna said.

"Yes. This is where I find myself when I have a lot of reading homework."

"Oh! So, you're a student." JoAnna said.

"Yes. A graduate student, majoring in Design. I want to become an Interior Decorator, have my own company one day.

"That sounds great." JoAnna said. "I just lost my mother and moved into the house I grew up in. I could use a little help with the decorating!"

"I'm so sorry about your mother." Melissa said. "Was it sudden?"

"Sort of. I made it here pretty much just in time."

The two talked for more than an hour.

"Well." Melissa said. "I guess I need to make it home and get ready for the day tomorrow."

"Ah! Me, too." JoAnna added.

Back in the car again, Melissa told JoAnna that they should 'do this again sometime.' JoAnna agreed.

"Let me drop you off at your car." Melissa said. JoAnna showed her where she had parked and smiled as she got out of the car."

"Hey!" Melissa said, giving JoAnna a slip of paper with her phone number. "Now you don't have to keep coming to the ticket window to see me."

"Was it that obvious?" JoAnna asked, blushing?

"Yes."

JoAnna drove home with every detail of the meeting with Melissa on her mind. "Yes, she thought to herself. I have a crush…I have a crush…on a young girl, a college girl!"

- CHAPTER 3 -

THE PROPOSAL

S omething had come alive in JoAnna. She smiled more and reached out to her neighbors and old friends, and some new friends that she was meeting through Melissa. She wanted to spend every moment of every day with Melissa but she was sure she was rushing the situation, and herself. She still had pangs of pain that occasionally creeped into her heart as she reminded herself that Liz had chosen to end their relationship rather than work on it. She wondered how deep their friendship could become and whether she'd risk heartbreak again. Should she keep her feelings to herself or just go for it!

"So, what do you like to do in your free time?" Melissa asked during one of their two-hour phone conversations.

"I don't know." JoAnna said. "I'm pretty much a home body. I like to watch tv and movies; mostly biographies. I like reading…oh! I like jigsaw puzzles, not the big ones but the kind you can finish in a day. What about you?"

"I guess I'm a 'people person', I love being around my friends and cooking for them. I like to listen to music. My parents say that I'm an 'old head' because I like classical and music from back in the day."

"So, you can cook?" JoAnna asked.

"Yes, and I'm pretty good at it." Melissa answered.

"Hmm. I should invite you over to cook…and to look at this place of mine. It's full of my mother's and father's things; their style. Maybe you can help me to spruce up the place."

"I would love to." Melissa said, excitedly. "When?"

"When?" JoAnna asked.

"Yes, when?" Melissa repeated.

"How about this weekend?" JoAnna asked. "Which day is best for you?"

"Saturday." She responded. "I'll stop by after work. Oh, and don't worry about shopping. I'll do all of that."

"I live on Alabaster Court; second house on the right."

JoAnna hung up the phone and giggled. She was so excited and could hardly wait for Saturday. She busied herself with school stuff, movies on tv and phone calls with Melissa. It was apparent that the two were drawing closer to each other and JoAnna was very happy that they were.

"I hope you like Italian!" Melissa said as she burst into the kitchen, arms filled with grocery bags.

"Sure." JoAnna said, moving out of her way. "I'm not hard to please."

JoAnna sat in the kitchen as Melissa prepared the meal and set the dinner table for two.

"This is delicious!" JoAnna said as she lifted her glass of wine for a toast. "You really are a great cook."

"I told you!" Melissa said. "Now, let's look at this house!"

Melissa walked slowly through the house with JoAnna, from room to room soaking up ideas for the house. When the two finally reached the living room, they sat on the couch together as Melissa shared her ideas.

"Sounds great!" JoAnna said.

"Well, I'm so glad you like the ideas." Melissa said. "I'll get started on them right away. Another excuse to see you."

"You don't need any excuses." JoAnna said, looking deep in her eyes. You are welcome here anytime."

Melissa leaned over to kiss JoAnna and she responded. The relationship had reached another plateau and both were invested in it.

Throughout the following months Melissa spent lots of time at JoAnna's house, cooking dinner and working on re-designing it as well as just being with JoAnna. The two went out to restaurants, movies and even ice skating during the winter in downtown Lexington. It would not be long before JoAnna finally asked Melissa to move in with her.

"Yes! Of course, I'll move in with you!" She answered. "I was wondering when you were going to ask me!"

Moving day came, finding JoAnna and Melissa working tirelessly getting all of Melissa's belongings in her new home.

"I thought you might like to turn the downstairs den into an office for you." JoAnna said. "There's plenty of room."

Melissa was so happy about the idea, and so was JoAnna.

It had been almost one year since that fateful meeting between JoAnna and Melissa at the Singletary Center. It was winter again and snow was falling down and temperatures were freezing.

"I've got an idea for a cold, dreary evening." Melissa told JoAnna. "Let's snuggle up in a blanket, warm ourselves with hot chocolate and put a jigsaw puzzle together! I just got a new one today."

"Sounds like a winner to me." JoAnna agreed.

Melissa prepared the hot chocolate and scrambled up the pieces of the jigsaw puzzle while JoAnna brought the blanket for the two of them.

"What is this puzzle?" JoAnna asked.

"You'll see." Melissa said. "It's only 300 pieces. We can put this together in one night."

JoAnna was a little suspicious but she went along with the events of the evening. After several hours, the puzzle began to take shape and eventually the words 'WILL YOU MARRY ME' appeared in the midst of red roses. JoAnna was in shock as she turned to Melissa.

"Well?" Melissa said, reaching behind the pillow on the couch to bring out a small box. She opened the box where two 'promise' rings were. She reached for JoAnna's hand and placed one of the rings on her finger.

"Of course, I will marry you!" JoAnna said, reaching for the other ring and placing it on Melissa's finger. The two kissed and snuggled up in the warmth of the blanket.

- CHAPTER 4 -

THE WEDDING

Melissa graduated from the University of Kentucky with her master's degree in Design that April. JoAnna was so proud of her. They celebrated with a quiet dinner for just the two of them at one of their favorite restaurants. Melissa hung her diploma up proudly in the downstairs office where all of her materials were. JoAnna surprised her with a sign for her office that read 'Designs by Melissa'.

"So, two months from now we will be married! I want you to feel free to plan the entire wedding." JoAnna told Melissa. "I have no idea where to start!"

It was obvious that Melissa knew exactly what to do to plan their wedding. It was agreed upon that the wedding would be held in their back yard since it would be Summer, and all of their family, friends and neighbors would be invited. Melissa began with the wedding gowns, suggesting that they visit wedding shops to look for just the right gowns and head pieces.

JoAnna did, however, suggest that their best friends, Pete and Freddie, be the ones to escort them down the aisle. The two had recently been married in Las Vegas after thirty-years being together, now living in Indiana. Both Pete and Freddie were very happy to have been asked and began making their plans to be in Lexington for the wedding. Melissa was extremely excited.

The two picked out their wedding rings together at a local jewelry store and headed toward the court house where they would obtain their Marriage License. Melissa chose a caterer that was recommended by one of her friends and a Minister that another friend suggested. Melissa chose decorations from the various shops in the city and stored them in the spare bedroom in the basement.

The weekend prior to the wedding, JoAnna and Melissa went from house to house on Alabaster Court inviting their neighbors to the wedding. From the Eliason's all the way around the court to the Blackwell's that had not been in their house for very long. They brought one calla lily for each household to announce their wedding. Everyone was excited for JoAnna and Melissa, accepted the calla lily and assured them that they would be there or at least try to be…that is except for Mark and Carol Kavanaugh.

"We'll be busy." Carol Kavanaugh said, refusing to take the calla lily. It was extremely apparent that she did not approve of JoAnna's and Melissa's marriage.

"Don't let it bother you." JoAnna told Melissa. "There's always one in the group. Just think of the ones that said they would try to come."

The Friday night before the wedding, Melissa and several of her girlfriends began decorating the deck and the backyard. Melissa insisted that JoAnna not go to the back door nor look out of the kitchen window. She wanted everything to be a surprise. JoAnna agreed and spent her time getting her nails and hair done while the decorating was going on. She was also responsible for picking up the wedding gowns, the calla lily bouquets and overseeing the cake and the catering. When night came, both were exhausted from all the preparations.

"I love you." Melissa said. She rolled over and was fast asleep before JoAnna could kiss her goodnight.

Morning came fast. Both JoAnna and Melissa rushed around the house putting their final touches on the day. Pete and Freddie can in early that morning. Melissa's friend picked them up at the airport and settled them in the guest room. After settling in, the two served as ushers, showing guests where to go to get to the back yard. By noon, another friend of Melissa's appeared with her makeup kit in tow.

Before long, the time had come for the two brides to make their appearance. When they met in the dining room, both had tears swelling in their eyes. Pete and Freddie took their places at the bottom of the stairs going down from the deck from where they would walk JoAnna and Melissa to the Minister. Once at the top of the deck, they could see their families, friends and all of their neighbors, except, of course, for the Kavanaughs. The back yard was beautiful! Melissa had rented a large tent where the reception would be held.

The music began to play through a speaker that was set up from the inside. JoAnna recognized it as a classical piece that Melissa played a lot. The two stood at the top of the stairs, smiling, giving their guests the opportunity to 'ooh and ahh' at how beautiful they looked. Pete and Freddie extended their hands as a sign that it was time to walk down the stairs. Once at the bottom, Pete took JoAnna and began to walk her toward the Minister and took his place beside her. Then Freddie did the same for Melissa, walking her to her father who gave her hand to JoAnna. Freddie took his place next to Melissa.

"Brothers and sisters…" The Minister said. "We are here today to join JoAnna O'Neill and Melissa Edwards together."

He continued with the standard wedding passages as JoAnna and Melissa wiped the tears away from their eyes. The two had written their own wedding vows and shared them at the appropriate time. Both ended their vows with "And I will love you forever."

"Ladies, you may now kiss your bride!"

Everyone in the back yard clapped as the two kissed. After hugging their guests, JoAnna and Melissa led the way to big tent for the reception. After dinner, JoAnna and Melissa prepared to throw their bouquets out into the crowd. They turned around and at the count of three, threw the bouquets and into two ladies' hands. There were toasts and speeches, music and dancing for well into the night. No one seemed to want to go home!

At the stroke of midnight, a limousine drove up to the front of the house. The guests made a long tunnel for the brides to run through as they made their way to the limousine that would take them to the airport for their flight to Barbados. There were tears of joy, balloons and plenty of good wishes.

Once inside the limousine, Melissa leaned over to kiss JoAnna.

"Thank you!" She said.

"For what?" JoAnna asked.

"Everything!"

BOOK V

The Eliasons

- Chapter 1 -

Henry, Betty and the Children

Eighteen-year-old Henry Eliason raised his hand and swore to '*...defend the Constitution of the United States against all enemies, foreign and domestic,...*' to enlist in the US Army. College had never been his first choice for life after graduation. Being from a small town in Ohio, his greatest desire had always been to 'see the world' and come back home after retirement from whatever job he had secured. He had thought of Trade School but was swept away by the young soldier that had come to his high school. The promise of higher education, a profession plus a salary sounded just too good to let slip away. It was right after graduation that Henry would find himself at the local Recruiter's Office listening to all that was available to him; and all for free.

Henry's parents made no secret of their disappointment over his choice. His high school sweetheart, Elizabeth Francis, known as 'Betty,' was devastated as well but would certainly wait for him no matter where the Army would send him.

Both Betty and Henry's mom cried as they watched him board the bus that would take him to Fort Knox, Kentucky for eight weeks of boot camp. It was a very somber moment, even for Henry's father, but not for Henry. He waved out the window until he could not see them anymore. The excitement was just overwhelming to Henry and he began to smile.

Everyone was right. Shortly after boot camp Henry received Orders to Vietnam, a thirteen-month tour of duty as a Radio Operator, the occupation he chose and qualified for. While in Vietnam, the letters were few and far in between but Betty understood and wrote to Henry everyday that he was gone. In one of the letters that Betty did receive from Henry was a marriage proposal. Both Betty's and Henry's parents insisted that the two waited until their twenty-first birthdays before they should even consider marriage. That, of course, did not stop Henry from buying an engagement ring once he was back home again.

Henry's first assignment after returning from Vietnam was with the 82nd Airborne in North Carolina. He turned twenty-one the next year and asked Betty to move to North Carolina when she turned twenty-one three months later. She began to pack the moment she read the letter and was on the bus to North Carolina the very day she turned twenty-one.

The two moved into military housing and set up housekeeping. Henry left for work every morning at 7:30 while Betty scanned the newspaper everyday looking for jobs on the Post or in the city just outside the Post and was able to get a job at the Thrift Shop on the Post and worked as a Cashier.

Six-months into their marriage, Betty began to feel very sick. She began vomiting, had hot flashes and felt very weak. She made her way to the doctor's office where she underwent several tests.

"Congratulations, Mrs. Eliason." The doctor told her. "You're pregnant. I would say about twelve-weeks along."

Betty was so excited that she couldn't wait for Henry to get home.

"This is wonderful news." Henry said, just as excited, holding her tight.

Daniel Henry Eliason, named after Betty's father and Henry, Sr., came into the world weighing 7lbs. 4oz., 19 ½ inches long. Both mother and son were doing well. Betty and Danny had to stay in the hospital for five days while Henry visited them as often as he could. When it was time for them to go home, Henry was there with baby clothes to change into. Once at home, 'Danny', as Henry and Betty chose to call him, was placed gently in his bassinette while they watched him sleep.

Danny was almost three-years-old when Henry received Orders to Virginia. It was a bittersweet goodbye for Betty, leaving her job and the friends that she had made in North Carolina. Henry felt the same way but was excited to move to another place as he was still anxious 'to see the world'. They moved into their military house and within several weeks after moving to Virginia, Betty would find out that she was pregnant again. They were both happy about the news because both Henry and Betty wanted a large family, plus they didn't want Danny to grow up alone.

Grace Elizabeth, named after Henry's mom and her mother, Betty, was born on a rainy night. She weighed 6lbs. 13oz., 20 inches long. Henry and Betty loved her dearly but it was three-year-old Danny that carried out his big-brother chores to help their mom take care of Grace. Danny insisted on sitting on Betty's lap when she rocked baby Grace in the rocking chair and loved napping in his toddler bed while she was asleep in her crib.

Danny entered Kindergarten when he was five-and-one-half-years-old and Grace was three-years-old and in the day care center on the Post. Betty decided to go back to work and took a job as a Teller at a local Bank in the small town outside of the Post. The Bank provided training and the opportunity for Betty to grow in the company. Within the next year, Henry and Betty were able to move from their military house into a house of their own.

Working for the Bank gave Betty the opportunity to meet some of the military wives from the Post and some of the wives of civilian employees from the local town. She was very happy with her loving husband, her new job, new home and their two children.

When Betty found out that she was pregnant for the third time, she also found out that she had gestational diabetes and was placed on a diet. During her third trimester, Betty became sick at work. She called Henry at work and told him that she was going home. Once laying down at home, she began experiencing cramps. She called Henry at work again and before she knew it, he was at home with her.

"I'm afraid I'm in labor, but it's too soon!" Betty told Henry. "I'm scared."

"Don't be scared, honey. "I'm here with you." Henry answered as he called the hospital.

He explained to the triage nurse that Betty had gestational diabetes and was having cramps, about three minutes apart. The nurse told Henry to bring Betty in. Their next-door neighbor had become good friends with Henry and Betty so Henry felt comfortable running next door to ask them to pick Danny and Grace up after school at the day care center where they both would be. The neighbors said 'of course'.

Henry carried Betty to the car and gently laid her in the front seat and began to speed down the road that led to the Post. Once at the Gate, Henry told the guard that his wife was in labor. The guard waved him through and called the hospital to let them know that Henry and Betty were on the way. A nurse was waiting with a wheelchair at the door to the emergency room when Henry drove up.

"I'm just going to park the car and I'll be right back." Henry told Betty. "I'll be right back!"

When Henry returned to the emergency room, Betty was hooked up to the baby monitor.

"I'm going to check her now to see if she's in full labor." The nurse said to Henry. Betty was crying and let out a scream with each labor pain. He held her hand as the nurse told them that Betty had dilated to seven; she was in full labor.

"Oh no!" Betty said, crying. "It's too soon!"

"It's okay." "Henry said, wiping her forehead with a towel. "I'm here, and the doctor should be on his way. Don't worry."

The doctor appeared shortly and tried his best to comfort and assure Betty and Henry that everything was going as it should be.

"You're moving along quite well so we'll just keep you comfortable and see how it goes."

Hours later, as the nurse was monitoring Betty's progress, the doctor appeared again and told Betty that she was going to need a C-Section because the baby was not turning so that the head was in the canal.

"A C-Section!" Henry said, anxiously. "How dangerous is that?"

"It'll be just fine." The doctor said as the nurse prepped Betty for the C-Section.

Betty was moved from the labor room to the operating room, Henry was close behind. Once inside, the doctor told Henry to stand at Betty's head. He held her hand as a tear flowed from her eye. The nurse draped her from the chest down as the doctor administered the anesthesia just prior to performing the C-Section. Betty went off to sleep as the doctor brought her baby girl into the world. The baby was checked and weighed before being put in the incubator.

"It's a girl!" The nurse said. "A big girl…8lbs. 7ozs., 21 inches long."

Henry went to the incubator. Smiling, he put his finger in her hand. The baby began to scream.

"Good lungs!" The nurse said. Henry smiled.

Henry followed Betty as she was wheeled into her room. She was sleeping peacefully as Henry sat by her side. It would be a couple of hours before she woke up and asked for the baby.

"It's a girl, honey, and she's just perfect. Just like Danny and Grace. I'll go get her now."

Henry ran down the hallway and came back with the baby in a rolling bed.

He placed the baby in Betty's arms.

"Oh! my goodness!" Betty said, kissing her on the forehead. "She's beautiful. What should we call her?"

"I like the name Meghan." Henry said smiling.

"Meghan…I like that, too." Betty said. "What about a middle name?"

"Anne!" Henry said. "What about Anne?'

"Meghan Ann Eliason." Betty said. "I love it!"

Henry and Betty decided at the birth of their third child that three was enough and they would not try to have anymore. Henry was afraid that another child would be too harsh on Betty, and she agreed.

CHAPTER 2

GROWING UP

Military life had proven itself to be quite fruitful for the Eliason's. With the exception of the occasional temporary tours of duty that only lasted a few months, the Army had managed to keep the family together.

Daniel was starting high school and contemplating his future. He considered being a dentist but also considered following Henry's footsteps and joining the Army. Henry explained that he could do both.

"The Army will put you through dental school when you serve." Henry said, proudly. "You have nothing to lose and everything to gain! But you have a few years to think about it, so take your time and make the best decision you can."

And that Daniel did, and in the end, he decided to attend the University of Ohio in Athens and joined ROTC as well. By the time Daniel was twenty-two-years-old, he had graduated from college with a degree in Biology and was ready to raise his hand to join the Army as a Second Lieutenant. Henry was so proud of him while Betty cried just as Henry's mother had cried those many years ago.

Daniel was stationed in Georgia for boot camp and then on to dental school.

His first two years after dental school were spent in Korea where he was promoted to First Lieutenant. He loved the Army and he loved taking care of his comrade's dental needs and he was, just like his father, excited to see the world. After Korea, Daniel spent one-month at home with his family before moving on to his next assignment in Germany. He loved being in Europe and travelled to London, Milan and Paris during his off times, sending beautiful gifts to Henry, Betty and his sisters.

During his various tours of duty and his free time overseas, Daniel dated but nothing serious. He had not left a high school sweetheart back home, in fact, Daniel's experience with girls while in school was few and far in between. At this time in his life, he was quite satisfied, however, to serve his country and to just casually date.

Middle child, Grace, had no plans to go to College nor did she have any plans for a future career. To Henry's and Betty's dismay, Grace proved to be their problem child. She would sneak out of her bedroom window to meet her friends or go to parties she was told that she could not go to as well as skip school. Henry had put his foot down with Grace too many times to count. She had been grounded so many times, and confined to her room that her parents rarely saw her.

Once she graduated from high school, Henry and Betty gave her the option of finding a job or moving out of their house. Fortunately for Grace, she was able to find a job at the Mall working at a clothing store where she received a discount for her personal purchases. She was definitely the best dressed young woman in the Mall.

Grace's life made a three-hundred-and-sixty-degree turnabout when she met a young man named Adam Peterson when she was twenty-two years old. She was able to buy a car and Henry agreed to put her on his insurance as long as she paid for it. Grace agreed and found herself travelling from wherever they were living to Kentucky to spend time with Adam who was a student at the University of Kentucky studying business administration at the time.

It would be at a derby party in Cincinnati, Ohio after the big race that the two would meet. Adam was standing in a corner with several friends of his staring at Grace and her friends.

"Take a picture it'll last longer!" She yelled out, laughing.

Adam smiled back at her. Before the night was over the two had exchanged phone numbers and made plans to see each other again soon. In the meantime, there would be long telephone calls between Grace and Adam or with one of her friends to talk about Adam. During one of their conversations, Adam asked Grace what her plans were for her future.

"I don't make plans." She answered. "I'm a spur of the moment kind of a girl. You know…"

"No. I don't." Adam said. "We have to have goals for our life, don't you think?"

"I've gotten along this long without them." Grace answered.

"What do you like to do?" Adam continued with his investigation.

"I don't know." Grace answered. "I like to sew."

"Well, there you go!" Adam replied, excited.

"I have to alter most of my clothes so I've learned a lot about sewing." Grace continued. "I guess it's a talent."

"Maybe you should design clothes or alter clothes for other people."

"I don't know…maybe." Grace shrugged. "I guess so."

"See?" Adam said. "That could be a plan!"

The two laughed but their conversation would soon be a conversation between Grace and her parents.

"You want to be a seamstress?" Betty asked.

"I guess so." Grace answered. "I know I'm really good at sewing. I could make a living at that, couldn't I?"

"I'm sure you could." Betty answered. "I'm sure you could."

Betty and Henry were just happy that their daughter was finally growing up and making some sort of plan for her future. She began to alter or repair clothes for her friends who spread the word that brought in additional work for her. She even designed a few outfits for friends for their special occasions.

Adam and Grace began to see each other seriously the next year after his graduation from the University. Grace visited with Adam's family in Lexington and he visited with Henry and Betty as well. The two eventually made plans to be married once Adam completed studies for his Master's the next year.

Grace's wedding would bring Daniel home on leave. Henry and Betty were so happy and proud to see their son in his Army uniform wearing the grade of Captain. Grace and Meghan were just thrilled to see their big brother and to open the gifts that he brought from his travels in Europe…a beer Stein for Henry from Germany; a German cookbook for Betty; a lovely silk fan for Meghan from Italy and fabric for Grace from Paris. It was a wonderful homecoming.

Grace and Adam's wedding, which was held at a local Church in Lexington, was also wonderful. Both Henry and Daniel walked Grace down the aisle and Meghan stood as her maid of honor. Henry and Betty cried as did Meghan and Grace as the two were presented to the Church as Mr. and Mrs. Adam Peterson.

Meghan's high school graduation left Henry and Betty with an empty nest. Meghan accepted the invitation from the University of Kentucky to start there the following Fall. She would major in Informational Technology, hoping to learn all she could about computers and grow in knowledge as they grew in everyday use.

Meghan was the baby of the Eliason family. She was quiet, spoiled and stuck like glue to her family. She cried for days when Daniel left for the Army and even wrote daily letters to him for the first few years. She chose to attend the University of Kentucky because Grace and Adam would be in Lexington and she would be close to Fort Knox where her parents were now living.

Meghan's boyfriend was not happy in the least when she left for Lexington but promised to be faithful while she was gone. She took the same pledge and hopped the bus to Lexington. College life was the perfect life for Meghan she realized as she went from class to class. She didn't even mind the homework or having to stay up half the night to study for a test. She liked her roommate, her classmates and most of her professors. She hopped the bus again on weekends to visit her parents. Laundry, homecooked meals and friendly, family conversation took the spotlight while Meghan was at home.

Meghan was in the campus Subway one afternoon during her sophomore year when she caught sight of a young man sitting at a table across from her. He was rather handsome, tall and alone. When he looked up, as if he knew she was staring at him, he nodded his head hello…she smiled and returned the nod. She suddenly remembered that she had seen him before, around the campus, working with a construction crew. He'd seen her, too, because he began to stare at her. By the end of Meghan's meal, the young man was gathering his belongings and met her at the door.

"Would you like to share my umbrella?" He asked a stunned Meghan. "It's raining now."

She had been so caught off guard by the young man that she didn't notice that it was raining.

"Hi." He said, extending his hand. "I'm Max…Max Douglas. What's your name?"

"Meghan." She answered. "It really is raining, isn't it? But thank you, no, my dorm is right across the street."

"Let me walk you…across the street." Max said, calmly. "I'm one of the good guys." He added.

"I don't doubt that." Meghan stated. "But I'm sure I won't melt."

She quickly ran out of the door and toward her dorm. Max watched her as if he was her guard for the night. She could still see his silhouette in the doorway to Subway from her dorm and she liked what she saw.

Meghan would notice Max more often on campus as she walked to her classes. He always acknowledged her with a nod of his head and she returned his acknowledgement with a smile. Eventually, Max would ask for her phone number and soon they would begin to date.

- CHAPTER 3 -

TIED UP LOOSE ENDS

The years passed by and found Henry celebrating his 28th year in the Army. Retirement was just around the corner and his final Orders read as his first Orders read…Fort Knox, Kentucky. It had been a long time since the family had been moved, but like Betty said, 'it will be the last move'. Over the years Henry had moved his family to many Army Posts from North Carolina to Texas, from New York to Indiana and even a one-year tour of duty in Korea when he left Betty and the girls stateside. He had worked on Air Force Bases and even had a temporary duty in Colorado. It had been an illustrious career and leaving it would be bittersweet. The plan was to move back to their home in Ohio once Henry retired. The house in Ohio had been sold years before so finding a new house was the task at hand.

The final two-years flew by for the empty nesters. Once home in their new house in Ohio, Henry and Betty enjoyed their retirement years fishing and visiting their daughters in Kentucky.

Daniel was now stationed in California providing dental services for the many soldiers that came in to his clinic. He loved being in California but missed his life in Europe. Daniel made his way home as often as he could to spend as much time with his parents as was possible, and even sent for them to visit him more than once.

Grace and Adam were living in Lexington after Adam accepted a job. Grace opened up a sewing shop in their spare bedroom and began taking orders for alterations and anything else that could be sewn; curtains, pillows, repairs and even her own clothing line. The two enjoyed having their friends over for outdoor bar-be-ques during the summer and cozy visits by the fireplace during the winter months. They, too, spent as much time as they could with Henry and Betty and always encouraged them to visit their home in Lexington.

Meghan and Max dated a couple of years before becoming a serious couple. She was more concerned about her education and put all of her attention and energy into her studies. Meghan worked hard to complete her master's degree and also attended follow-up classes to keep up with the growing computer demand. As for Max, he continued working for the University for a few years until he made the decision to start his own business as a 'handy man', providing services for individuals rather than institutions.

When Max finally asked Meghan to marry him, he also made the statement that he wanted 'lots of kids', enough to build a basketball team. Meghan was extremely hesitant about having children and told Max that they would have to wait awhile.

"I had goals set for myself before I met you." Meghan said to Max. "I have to be true to myself and right now having kids is out of the question."

"So, when do you think you'll be ready?" Max asked.

"I can't answer that now." Meghan answered. "Please don't put me on the spot."

Despite their difference in opinion about having children, Meghan and Max were married on a lovely spring day in May. Henry and Betty were excited for the two and made the trip to Kentucky to attend the wedding. Grace stood as Meghan's maid of honor. It was a small gathering particularly on Max's side since both of his parents had passed away. Meghan invited her best friends from all of the places that she had lived with her parents as well as her family members. Daniel was able to fly to Kentucky from California on leave to also attend the wedding. Just as with Grace, Henry and Daniel walked Meghan down the aisle together.

The two moved into a small apartment near Alabaster Drive and set up housekeeping. Meghan was able to find employment as an IT Specialist at a local bank and Max was finally ready to start his own handy man business. The conversation about having children came up often which caused frequent arguments between the two. Meghan discussed the situation with her mother.

"Like you said, Meghan, you had set goals for yourself long before you met Max." Betty told her daughter.

"And now I have my dream job!" Meghan said. "I just think kids should come when both husband and wife decide to have them."

"You're right, honey." Betty said. "I was ready, but it was a different time when your father and I were married."

"By the way." Meghan said, changing the conversation. "There's a house for sale on Alabaster Court, just up the road from us. Please tell me you'll think about moving to Kentucky! I miss you and dad so much! This house is perfect for you and dad."

"We'll see." Betty said. "We miss you, too."

As fate would have it, the house on Alabaster Court remained vacant while Meghan had the same conversation with her mother over and over again about them moving to Kentucky. It would not be long before Grace joined in the conversation and not long after that that Henry and Betty would make the trip to look at the house on Alabaster Court.

"We'll take it!" Henry said, agreeing with Betty that this would be the perfect house for them, plus they would be close to Grace and Meghan. The two moved into the house at 11741 Alabaster Court, on the corner of the court and Alabaster Drive, and were welcomed by Pat Davis and the calico cat that roamed the court. They were less than one-mile from Meghan and Max.

Meghan was awakened in the middle of the night by a voice coming from the bathroom just off their bedroom. It was Max. He was on the phone speaking in a very low voice.

"Who are you talking to?" Meghan asked.

Max turned around to come face-to-face with Meghan who was standing in the doorway.

"I asked you who you're talking to at this time of the night?"

"It's a customer." Max said, putting his hand over his phone. "We're talking about a job she needs done; it's a big job that will bring in plenty of money. This was the only free time she had to call. Besides, it's an area that's an hour behind us. Go back to bed. I'll tell you all about it in the morning."

Meghan tossed what Max had said around in her head, suspecting that there was more to the situation than he was telling her. In the coming months, Max would come home later and later, and was unavailable on his phone quite often. He always had an excuse as to why he was not available.

"Look, Meghan, my job is not like yours. I don't work a nine-to-five job. I have deadlines to meet!" Max said in the middle of an argument.

"Are you seeing somebody else?" Meghan asked point blank one night.

"Why would you ask me something like that?"

"Because I believe you are!" Meghan answered. "There's nothing you can say that will convince me otherwise."

"Well, if there's nothing I can say to convince you otherwise…"

"You really are having an affair!" She said angrily. "Aren't you?"

There was silence.

"All I wanted was a baby and you wouldn't give me that." Max shouted.

"You wanted a basketball team!" Meghan shouted back. "So, is she giving you a baby?"

Silence again.

"Oh my gosh! She's pregnant, isn't she?"

"Meghan, please…"

"No. Don't come near me." Meghan said, walking toward the bedroom. She began to pack a small bag.

"Where are you going?" Max asked.

"None of your business." She answered.

She grabbed the bag, her toothbrush and drove to her parents' house. Henry and Betty opened the door and their arms. It had only been five years since their wedding and now Meghan was seeking a divorce for irreconcilable differences. She moved into her parents' spare room and continued to move her things from the apartment while Max was at work. She cried for days, even blaming herself at one point.

"No, honey." Betty said. "You can't blame yourself for any of this. You told him exactly who you were before you married him. So, you have nothing to blame yourself for. Now, you need to start your life over…fresh!"

Meghan became friends with Charlotte Davis, Pat's daughter and began to feel 'fresh' as her mother said she would.

Two years after the Eliason's moved to Alabaster Court, Henry Eliason died of a massive coronary. Betty, Grace and Meghan were at his side in the house as they waited for the ambulance. Pat Davis came across the court to offer food, comfort and anything else she could do to help. Betty was overcome with grief as were Grace and Meghan. Grace immediately contacted Daniel who was able to take emergency leave to come home. Grace picked him up at the airport while Meghan and Pat stayed home with Betty. It was the saddest of times that the family had ever experienced.

With the help of Daniel and the survival officer from Fort Knox, Henry was flown to Arlington National Cemetery in Virginia. Betty, Grace and Adam with their three children joined Meghan and Daniel for the long drive to Arlington where he received a twenty-one- gun salute with the slow, melodic sounds of Taps. Betty received the ceremonial flag on behalf of the family. Henry was buried twelve feet deep with six-feet above reserved for Betty when it was her time.

Two months after the death of Henry Eliason, Daniel received Orders to Afghanistan. Betty was devastated, to say the least. Daniel flew out of California to Kentucky before his departure to Afghanistan, spending one-week with the family before shipping out.

"Promise you'll come home safely." Betty said with tears flowing down her cheeks.

"I'll be fine, mom." Daniel replied. "I promise. You take care of yourself."

That following summer, Charlotte Davis was found floating in her parents' backyard pool. It was such a shock to all of the residents the night the lights and sirens blasted their way down Alabaster drive and into the Court. When Betty realized that the problem, whatever it was, was happening at the Davis' house, she ran across the Court to be with her friend Pat. It was a disturbing time.

Daniel Eliason, Jr. was born to Daniel, Sr and Jennifer Parker Eliason on May 8, 2017 in Louisville, Kentucky. Jennifer, an Army Reservist, had been Daniel's dental hygienist while in Afghanistan. The two had begun to have long conversations between patients and, after finding so much in common, fell in love. Daniel would leave Afghanistan ahead of Jennifer with Orders to Arizona. She would arrive at her destination with Orders to Georgia several months later. The two would have a long-distance relationship for about a year, visiting each other whenever possible but filling the lonely hours with very long phone calls. They would quietly marry.

Just like his father, Henry Eliason, Daniel was stationed at Fort Knox, Kentucky near the time for his retirement. Jennifer would retire from the Reserves a few years later. The two would begin to work at a Dental Clinic in Louisville, Kentucky shortly after Jennifer retired. The owner of the clinic died suddenly and his family allowed Daniel and Jennifer to buy out the clinic which was then called 'Eliason Family Dentistry'. Daniel and Jennifer visited Betty and his sisters often.

Grace and Adam bought a house on the other side of town to accommodate their growing family, but remained close to Betty and Meghan with frequent visits. Grace began having Sunday dinners for the family at the new house and everyone would attend. Betty enjoyed being with her children and her grandchildren at the dinners. It was always a time of kinship and remembrance for all.

Book VI
The Kavanaugh's

IN THE BEGINNING

I n 1972, the city of Lexington gave permission for a new housing area to be developed in the south end. The new housing area would provide easier access to the downtown area, the University of Kentucky as well as shopping centers and gas stations. Mark Kavanaugh was an English professor at the university at the time the area was being developed for potential tenants to purchase property and build their future homes. Carol, his wife, was happy to be a stay-at-home mom to their children. When the land finally went up for sale, Mark and Carol were one of the very first to visit the new area and the first to build their new home.

Since the street adjacent to the new area was Alabaster Drive, it was only fitting and proper to name the court that emptied into the drive, Alabaster Court. Mark and Carol, along with their children, would drive across town every week to watch the progress as their house was being built. Carol enjoyed picking out the crown molding, lighting, colors, appliances and landscaping designs.

Shortly after the Kavanaugh house was about to be finished, several other houses were beginning to be built by the original owners. By the summer of 1973, five out of the seven houses in the court were completed and families were moving their furniture and personal items into their new homes. The land across the court from the Kavanaugh's and the land next door to them was still available. It occurred to Mark that the land across from them would be a perfect place to build a house for Mark's eldest sister, Kit, a manager for a local restaurant. Kit was divorced with two children and, as many single mothers find themselves, was struggling to make ends meet. Carol agreed that building a house for Mark's sister would alleviate the high cost of rent. Kit was overjoyed.

"I can't thank you both enough!" Kit said to Mark and Carol. "There is just no way that I can repay you for building a house for me and the kids."

"We're just glad we are able to do something to help you!" Carol said.

"I'm just so happy that you're not with that son-of-a-bitch of a husband of yours!" Mark said.

"Ex-husband!" Kit reminded Mark.

Kit was fifteen years older than Mark and had virtually raised him since both of their parents worked long hours. By the time Mark began kindergarten, Kit was already in college studying for her undergraduate's degree. She had always wanted to have a restaurant of her own in the middle of downtown Lexington but settled for being the manager of an elite restaurant that was already established. Kit worked for various retail outlets right after graduation from college but took a chance to apply for the manager's position and was thrilled to have gotten it.

Tom Everett, an Architect, wined and dined Kit after meeting her at the restaurant where he brought his business clients on a regular basis. Kit was struck by his business appeal as well as his good looks and generosity to her employees. Mark was always a little skeptical of Tom but tolerated him because of his love for his sister. The marriage lasted almost seventeen-years and ended with very little explanation. No one was exactly sure what had happened but Kit always said 'he was a wonderful father but a lousy husband.'

Alabaster Court was thriving. The land on the corner by the Kavanaugh's house was finally being built. Carol became friends with the

O'Neill's that lived next door to Kit and the Davises' that lived a few houses down. She made a vegetable garden in the back yard and shared her cucumbers, tomatoes and peppers with her neighbors. The Kavanaugh's yard was the prettiest yard in the court. Mark loved cutting his own grass and Carol loved planting flowers. There were fresh cut flowers on the dinner table everyday and crispy lettuce and juicy tomatoes from the garden.

The first Christmas on Alabaster Court was cold and snowy but beautiful with all of the holiday lights and Christmas trees in the windows. Carol, along with their children, baked and decorated sugar cookies while Mark delivered them in tiny Christmas boxes with ribbons to the residents of Alabaster Court.

Every Sunday morning and every Wednesday evening Mark and Carol would pack up their children and Kit's children and head over to their Church. On Mondays, Mark led a Bible Study in their home. Several of their friends from outside of Alabaster Court would also attend. There were no excuses for the family not to attend Church Services or Bible Study.

The oldest of the Kavanaugh children, Carolyn, graduated from middle school the next year and Corinne would be entering middle school when school began again; leaving the three youngest children, Catherine, Casey and Caleb not too far behind. Kit's children were older; Sarah, her oldest was nearly seventeen-years-old, and Kelly was fifteen-years-old when they moved into the house on Alabaster Court. Sarah was a senior in high school and began her last year at the nearby school. Kelly, a sophomore, attended the same school while Kit tended to the demands of the restaurant. The girls were home alone after school until Kit came home after the dinner crowd but were near enough to their Uncle Mark and Aunt Carol in case there was a problem.

Kit and her ex-husband, Tom Everett, had 'shared custody' of the girls which meant that Sarah and Kelly spent every other weekend with their dad and at least one day during the week. Tom lived not too far from

Alabaster Court which made it easy for the transfer. The girls would catch the bus from Kit's house to school and Tom would drive them to and from school.

Carol spent her days with her two youngest children, the only two boys, Casey four-years-old and Caleb three-years-old, teaching them the fundamentals such as the alphabet, numbers and colors in preparation for Kindergarten. Carol and Kit spoke to each other on the phone everyday and often times switched off having dinner at each other's house. Family and closeness were very important to the Kavanaugh's.

Professor 'K', as his students called him, was at the University at 7:30 each weekday morning. He would enjoy his cup of coffee in the teachers' lounge and scan the newspaper until his students began to enter the lecture hall. He was at home by 4:00pm sharp from the University every afternoon. Dinner was served by 5:30pm every evening except for Bible Study night when dinner was ready by 5:00pm since the Study began at 6:00pm. The extra half-an-hour gave the family time to clean up the kitchen and dining room, and prepare for their guests. Once the two boys were asleep, Mark and Carol enjoyed their time alone, watching tv, a movie or just being together.

CHAPTER 2

GROWING UP

The land on the corner of Alabaster Drive and the Court, next door to the Kavanaugh's house had finally been purchased and the house was being built. Everyone in the Court was waiting to see the owners, their furniture as it was being unloaded from the moving truck and what kind of automobile they would drive. Not many years after the family moved in, the moving truck was back in the driveway and the house was on the market. In fact, that particular house, over the many years that the Kavanaugh's lived on Alabaster Court, was home to three families prior to it being purchased by the Blackwell's that moved in after the murder of Charlotte Davis.

When Casey and Caleb finally went to Kindergarten, Carol took on another project to 'give back' to the community. Her father had been in the Army for many years and had been dead for many years. She always wanted to do something for the veterans so she signed up to volunteer at the Veteran's Administration Hospital for three days per week; Tuesdays, Wednesdays and Thursdays. She loved being with the veterans and made coffee several times each day to make sure they had coffee while they were waiting for their appointments. She also walked patients or pushed them in their wheelchairs to their appointments. Carol would drive the boys to school on the days she volunteered at the VA and pick them up.

"Have you heard from my sister today?" Mark asked Carol as they were at dinner one evening.

"No, actually, it's been a couple of days now." Carol answered. "I haven't talked to her since Monday night. Maybe I'll give her a call after dinner."

"Ok." Mark answered. "I'm sure everything is ok.

When dinner was finally over, Carol dialed Kit's number. The phone rang and rang but Kit did not answer.

"She may not be home from work yet." Carol said. "I'll try her again in about an hour if I haven't heard from her yet."

Kit still did not answer the phone when Carol called about an hour later. Both of Kit's daughters were now married and living out of state so it would be fruitless to call and alarm them. Mark looked out the front door and noticed that the lights were on at Kit's house.

"I'm going over there." Mark said, looking for the keys to Kit's house. "I'll be right back.

He walked across the court and knocked on the door to Kit's house. No one answered. After knocking several times, he finally decided to open the door and see for himself what was going on.

"Kit?" Mark yelled out.

There was no answer. He began to walk around the house and finally up the stairs yelling out her name. The door to her bedroom was closed so he knocked on the door. Still no answer.

Mark opened the door to the bedroom and there, on the floor on the side of the bed was his sister in her pajamas. Mark quickly checked the pulse in her neck. There was none. He called 911.

"I need help!" He yelled in the phone. "My sister…I think she's dead. Please, send an ambulance."

The next call he made was to Carol who immediately ran across the court to Kit's house.

"Oh! Dear God!" Carol said. "Is she dead?"

"I think so." Mark said. "I called 911."

The ambulance drove into the Court and parked in the front of Kit's house. Kit's body was placed on a gurney and loaded into the ambulance. Mark and Carol drove behind the ambulance to the hospital. Once at the emergency room, the doctor came out to announce that Kit had indeed passed away. Mark and Carol hugged each other as tears flowed down their cheeks.

"We need to call the kids." Carol said, reaching for her phone. "Why don't you call one and I'll call the other one?"

"Yes." Mark said. "I'll call Sarah."

Both girls were distraught.

"Have you called my dad?" Sarah asked Mark.

"You should do that, honey." Mark replied.

The autopsy revealed Kit died from a brain aneurysm and had likely been dead for two days. Both Mark and Carol were heartbroken thinking that they may have been able to save her if they had only gone to the house earlier.

Kit's funeral was delayed in order for her girls and their families to get to Lexington. It was a stormy day when she was laid to rest at her family Church. The Church was filled with people that were regulars at the restaurant that had come to bid their final farewells.

Kit's house was the next item of business. It went on the Market but rumor spread that the owner had died in the house so no one seemed to be interested in buying it.

"Well, Mark." Carol said. "Maybe we can rent it. After all, we live across the court and can certainly watch over the house where Kit lived."

"You're right." Mark replied. "I can even put a notice at the University. Maybe a faculty member would be interested."

The very next day Mark put the notice on the bulletin board in the English Department at the University. Several weeks passed without a phone call about renting the house. One afternoon the phone rang at Mark's desk. It was a student at the University interested in renting the house.

"There are four of us that are interested in renting the house." The voice on the other end of the phone said. "We will split the bills and take good care of the house."

"I'll have to get back to you." Mark said. "I need to discuss this with my wife. I'll call you this evening."

Carol was not so sure about having a bunch of young college students living in the house but Mark finally convinced her that it would not be a problem since the two of them would oversee the property. Mark made the phone call that evening to the young man and asked him to meet at the house to fill out the lease for six months.

"We'll see how this works out during these six months." Mark said. The young man agreed.

The following weekend Mark and Carol met with the young man and his three friends. They all walked through the house and then they all signed the six months lease. Within the week, the four young students were moving in the house with what seemed to be just bedroom furniture.

Most of the time it was quiet at the house where the young college students lived but occasionally there were parties that literally raised the roofs of the houses on Alabaster Court. Mark could be seen walking across the court at all hours of the day or night to 'lay down the law'. Eventually, Mark and Carol set the rules and informed the young men that any infringement could lead to an eviction.

Through the years there would be several groups of young men or young women that lived in the house. There came a time when the house was vacant for repairs around the time of Charlotte Davis's murder. It would not be long after the house repairs were completed that the notice was back on the bulletin board at the University and Mark's phone began to ring off the hook, young people calling to ask about the rental house on Alabaster Court.

It would be in the middle of a warm, summer's night that the flashing lights and the sirens came down Alabaster Drive into the court and awakened the Kavanaugh's. Mark slipped into his robe and made his way to the living room window, Carol followed close behind. He wasn't sure which house the police had gone to because the entire court was full of ambulances, fire trucks and police. But those that did not know at the time of Charlotte's death would find out the next day when the initial investigation began.

The Kavanaugh's five children were now either married, in college or just had moved away for their independence. When the grandchildren were born and began to spend summers with their grandparents, Mark put a basketball goal in the court for their enjoyment and invited the other children of the court to enjoy it as well. The young people in the rental house also enjoyed a friendly game of basketball every now and then.

Book VII
The Blackwell's

DIAGNOSIS

"Mrs. Blackwell, I do believe Peter has Attention Deficit/Hyperactivity Disorder, or ADHD." Mrs. Jones said. "He truly is having a tough time in class. I can make some recommendations for some doctors that specialize in this disorder."

"He's having a tough time at home as well." Mrs. Blackwell said. "He seems to be having trouble staying on task when he's doing homework, or he just fidgets, has trouble sitting still."

"That's exactly what's happening here, in school." Mrs. Jones continued. "Sometimes he blurts out answers when I ask the children to raise their hands before they speak or he stares out of the window when I am calling on him. ADHD is a lot more common than you would expect, and there are medicines that can help him."

"I don't want to make a zombie out of him." Mrs. Blackwell said. "I hear those kinds of medicines can be worse than the condition itself."

"I do understand but I'm not a doctor to speak to any of this really, but I do suggest that you contact a doctor as soon as you can."

"Of course. I'll do that today."

Mrs. Jones wrote down the names of several doctors that specialized in ADHD and Mrs. Blackwell made an appointment for the next week. After several tests, the doctor told Mrs. Blackwell that her nine-year-old son, Peter, did indeed have symptoms of ADHD and prescribed medication. Although the symptoms began to improve, Mrs. Blackwell's biggest concern materialized: Peter was drowsy most of the time and it was hard to wake him up in the mornings. After experimenting with various medications over a long period of time, Peter was finally able to function better with minimal side effects.

More tests revealed that Peter was also dyslexic. He was not less intelligent than his peers; he was just encountering more challenges to achieve the same success because of the disorder. Mr. and Mrs. Blackwell were very supportive of their young son and were willing to do whatever necessary to help him, especially when he became frustrated. They hired a young woman that specialized in reading techniques to aid children with Dyslexia and again Peter began to succeed.

Peter was an extremely talented child who loved building and repairing things, especially with Legos that allowed him to build, destroy and then repair Lego houses. The Blackwell's kept him busy as they subtly educated him and helped him to be educated at school. Once in High School, Peter became shy and reserve when he was with other people, especially his classmates. He told his parents that he felt 'odd' and compared himself to what he called 'normal' people. His parents struggled to help their son and at his high school graduation, Peter announced that he did not want to go to college; he wanted to go to a trade school that would teach him how to perform construction work, particularly plumbing.

"Okay." Peter's father said, delighted that he son at least was not dropping completely out of school. "We'll find something together."

And that they did. Mr. Blackwell was able to locate a construction company whose contract manager agreed to take Peter on as an apprentice. Peter worked with the man for a few years and was finally hired by a local plumber in Lexington. He was so happy to show off his skills and before long, Peter was going on calls all by himself.

As a young man, Peter went all over the city helping people with their plumbing needs. He was always available for weekend jobs or any time of the day or night for emergency calls. Peter met a young lady by the name of Amy on one of those emergency calls. Amy's mother called the service and Peter was on the job in a matter of minutes. The garbage disposal was not working at all so Peter volunteered to buy one at the local hardware store. It was apparent that there was a connection between the two and by the time the new garbage disposal was installed, Amy and Peter were having coffee with Amy's mother. From then on, Amy's mother called Peter whenever anything went wrong with the house. Amy was more than happy to see him and the two would soon start dating. Peter felt it was only fair to tell Amy about his ADHD. She was very concerned for Peter, and was even aware of the disorder and what it meant for him and her.

Two years later, Peter and Amy would marry and move into a small apartment. The next year the two began looking for a permanent house to purchase and stumbled upon the house on the corner of Alabaster Drive and Alabaster Court, the house next door to the Kavanaugh's. It was a 'fixer-upper', just the kind that Peter loved. By the time the house was just the way the Blackwell's wanted it, Amy was pregnant with their third baby girl.

- CHAPTER 2 -

THE RED SHOE

I t was a bright and sunny Summer day in Alabaster Court. Peter Blackwell was washing his car when a neighbor ran over; the neighbor was one of the students that lived at 11735. He seemed frantic when he approached Peter.

"We have a problem at the house." The student said excitedly. "There's black stuff coming up in the shower and it stinks something awful!"

Peter looked toward the house where all of the students were now standing outside on the front porch.

"That doesn't sound good." Peter said, shutting the hose off and wiping his hands on his shorts. "Just give me a minute; I'll be right with you."

Peter ran inside the house to get a dry tee-shirt and then across the Court to the students' house. Once inside, he could smell the odor.

"There's a broken pipe, I would say, causing sewage to come into the shower. Have you checked the garage?"

All of the students followed Peter into the garage. There, on the floor of the garage was a large puddle of sewage and water. The odor was much worse in the garage than it was in the bathroom.

"Don't touch anything," Peter said sternly. "I'll go get some tools and my camera. I can push the camera into the clean-catch and see where the broken pipe is."

Moments later he reappeared with a tool box and a long black cable. He made his way through the group of students to the clean-catch in the garage and inserted the cable with a small camera at the tip connected to a monitor. Once he turned on the system, he began to push the cable further and further through the pipes until he found the break…and what appeared to be a shoe that was stuck to one side of the broken pipe.

"I think we're going to have to dig up this entire area to replace the broken pipe after I turn the water off. The break looks to be between the garage and the manhole in the middle of the Court, but closer to the house." Peter shut the water off and looked from one of the students to the other. "Anybody know how a shoe got in there???" Peter asked angrily.

Everyone answered 'no'.

"I'll have to excavate the area along the front side of your house. And none of you know how a shoe got in there?"

Again, the answer was 'no'.

"In the meantime, you can clean up this mess." Peter said. "You can sweep the garage out and run hot water in the shower. Clean the shower and the garage floor with bleach." Peter continued. "I'll be back in a little while."

Peter suspected the students had caused the pipe break and that at least one knew something about the shoe. that showed up in the video that he had created. He quickly gathered a shovel and other tools including pipes that would fit the broken one and headed back over to the students' house. The smell of bleach and sewage filled the air, an almost choking odor. Peter put his mask on, grabbed the shovel and began to dig. After nearly an hour, Peter was able to locate the broken pipe, remove it and dislodge the shoe that was stuck to one side. He attached the new pipe and turned the water back on. Prior to filling the large hole with the dirt from the excavation, Peter lifted the shoe up in the air and asked for the third time, "Does anyone know where this shoe came from?" For the third time, the answer was 'no'.

As Peter was finishing the work, the student named Chuck was driving up to the house.

"What happened here?" He asked one of the other students as he exited his car.

"Busted pipe."

"Aw man!" Chuck replied. "Boy! Does it stink!"

"Let me ask you," Peter said as he washed the shoe with the hose. "do you have any idea why there was a shoe buried in the ground here?"

"No." Chuck replied, puzzled.

"Looks like it's been there for a long time." One of the students said.

"Like maybe seventeen-years?" Chuck asked, surprised. "Could this be the shoe that was missing in the Charlotte Davis murder case? What color is it?"

Peter examined the shoe and finally answered. "It's faded but it looks to be red, a red Converse tennis shoe."

"That's it!" Chuck said, excited. "The shoe that was missing is a red, Converse tennis shoe!"

"Well how the hell did it find its way in your yard?" Peter asked, holding the shoe up for inspection.

"All I know is that the house was empty during the time of the murder. The owner was having it remodeled. When I moved in, that was the story; the owner told me that it had been remodeled probably a decade before." Chuck answered. "I think we need to call the cops!"

Everyone was quiet until Peter remembered that the two Detectives had been by his house not long before to ask questions about the murder. One of them had given him a business card.

"I've got the Detective's business card somewhere in the house. I'll give him a call." Peter said.

"Okay." Chuck responded.

The students stood on the front steps of the house as Peter walked across the Court to his house with the shoe. He searched throughout the house for the business card and found it on his chest-of-drawers in the bedroom. Locating his cell phone, he called the number on the business card. The voice on the other end of the phone answered…

"Homicide Cold Case, may I help you?"

"Yes, this is Peter Blackwell." He replied. "I need to speak to a Detective Steve Martinez, please."

"Yes, one moment, please."

After a few moments, Steve Martinez answered the phone.

"Hello." Peter said. "This is Peter Blackwell. I live on Alabaster Court here in Lexington. I met with you recently. You were asking questions about the Charlotte Davis case. I think I may have some information for you about that case."

"Okay, Mr. Blackwell." Steve said, reaching for a pen and paper. "What have you got?"

"Well, I think I've found the missing shoe; a red Converse tennis shoe, right?" Peter asked.

"Yes!" Steve said excitedly. "Where is the shoe right now?"

"I have it right here in my hand." Peter answered calmly.

"Okay. I'll be there shortly."

Steve grabbed his jacket and his phone and headed out of the door.

"Hey Carl." He said after calling Carl on his cell phone. "Meet me at the Blackwell's house on Alabaster Court. I'm on my way there now. You won't believe what we may have!"

Steve pulled into the Blackwell driveway and waited for Carl, who parked along the curb in front of the house and got out of the car to meet Steve at the door to the Blackwell house.

"So, what's the 911?" Carl asked.

"Just wait, brother." Steve answered. I think we've hit the jackpot!"

Peter Blackwell opened the door to his house and invited the two Detectives inside.

"Please, have a seat." Peter said. He walked into another room of the house and reappeared with the shoe in his hand. "A red Converse tennis shoe!"

"Oh, my goodness!" Carl said. "Where on earth did you find this?"

"The house where the students live; they had a busted pipe and sure enough, the shoe was stuck in one side of the broken pipe. Nobody knew how it got there except the one that's been there the longest. I think he said his name is Chuck. He's the one that guessed it was the missing shoe from the Charlotte Davis case."

"Well, lookey here!" Steve said, picking up the shoe. "Charlotte was missing her left shoe and this is definitely a left shoe."

"So, do you think this is the shoe?" Carl asked.

"I would say so." Steve answered. "We'll certainly compare it to the one in the evidence box but to me, we now have evidence! Meet me at my office and we'll make the comparison."

The two detectives made their way to the Homicide Cold Case division and met in Steve's office. Carl's heart was pounding in his chest when he and Steve went into the Evidence Room to compare the two shoes.

"Yep! That's it!" Steve said excitedly as he held the two shoes up in the air. "Maybe we'll be lucky enough to find the object the perp used to hit Charlotte in the head."

"If the house was vacant in 2003 and repairs were being made," Carl said, pondering. "Is it possible that the perp could be a contractor or a handy man that was working on the house?"

"No doubt." Steve answered. "Let's find out who the company was that did the makeover on the house."

"Certainly, the property owner would have that information." Carl said.

"Let's get started." Steve said.

Carl agreed as he lifted the two shoes. "I never thought I'd be so excited about a shoe!"

- CHAPTER 3 -

FINDINGS

It was easy enough to learn the name of the construction company that had worked on the house where the students were now living; Coleman and Parkinson Contractors provided a complete crew in 2003 to completely remodel the house at 11735 Alabaster Court. The company was located just outside the Lexington city limits. Carl and Steve made plans to meet there the next day at 10:00am. The two were greeted by the Office Manager.

"May I help you?" The Office Manager asked.

"Yes." Steve answered after introducing himself and Carl. "We need to speak to someone about a construction crew that was working a job on Alabaster Court in 2003."

"I can help you with that. But may I ask what you need this information for?"

"We've re-opened a homicide case and recently found evidence from that case that pointed to a house that your company was remodeling back in 2003." Steve answered. "If you could help us…"

"Yes, of course." The Office Manager said. "Let me check the files and I'll be right with you. Please, have a seat."

The Office Manager disappeared into an office and returned momentarily with a file folder.

"Here's the list of the crew members that worked that job in 2003. I'll make a copy of it for you."

"We'd appreciate that." Steve said.

The Office Manager gave the copies to Steve. "That was seventeen years ago so this crew is not together anymore. Usually, crew members move on to the next job; could be local, could be out of town. The list will give you the addresses and phone numbers that we had where they lived in 2003. Unfortunately, that's all we have on that particular crew."

"That's fine." Steve said. "At least it's a start. Thank you for your time."

"Your office or mine?" Steve asked Carl as the two walked back to their cars.

"Let's make it yours." Carl answered. "I wouldn't want to find myself in the middle of a missing persons' case while in the middle of a murder case!"

"Smart idea." Steve said. "Meet you there."

Back at the Homicide Cold Case office, the two Detectives proceeded to examine the names on the list of construction crew members that had remodeled the house on Alabaster Court.

"There must be thirty names on this list!" Carl said. "What are we looking for?"

"I don't know yet." Steve said. "It'll pop out at us when we find it."

"So, are we going to interview each of the people on this list like we did the residents of Alabaster Court?" Carl asked.

"I sure hope not!" Steve answered. "That would take forever. We'll split up the list, call each one and find out what kind of information we can learn from the phone calls first. Then, if an interview is warranted, we'll make an appointment. Here, you take the first half."

The phone calls went on for what seemed like hours to no avail. Many of the 2003 construction crew had moved on, just as the Office Manager at Coleman and Parkinson had said, and several were no longer at the phone number that was listed.

"Wait a minute!" Carl said excitedly. "I think I found IT!"

"What?" Steve asked.

"Meghan Eliason-Douglas' husband's name is Max, I think." Carl said, looking through his notes. "Yes! Meghan's husband's name is Max and there is a Max Douglas on this list and the address listed is 249 Pine Hill Road, Apartment #9. He's listed as 'drywall'. That's the street just down from Alabaster Court. I remember seeing that street name because we passed it so often when we were interviewing the residents of Alabaster Court."

"I would say he's deserving of an interview!" Steve said with a smile.

"I'll be happy to drive!"

"Ya know," Carl said as they headed down the highway to the familiar area. "My money would be on Alex McKenzie, Brad Simmons or the guy in Florida that was bothering Charlotte Davis. But this guy…seems too obvious."

"Well, he could be the perfect perp; living in the area, working in the area and formally married to one of the residents of Alabaster Court." Steve said. "He also would have had access to an instrument that could cause blunt force trauma."

"That does sound logical, but why?" Carl asked.

"That's the key question." Steve answered. "Why?"

The car continued its journey to Pine Hill Road. Once there, the two Detectives exited the car and walked up the walkway to the apartment. They quickly found apartment #9. Steve knocked on the door. No one answered.

"He's probably working." Carl said.

"Perhaps." Steve said, knocking again. Still no answer. "Let's take a little trip to Betty Eliason's house. Meghan is probably still at work. I'm sure she has some information about her ex-son-in-law."

"Good idea." Carl added.

Steve drove the car into the driveway at Betty Eliason's house on the corner of Alabaster Court and Alabaster Drive. Betty was watering her flowers in the front yard when the two Detectives made their presence known.

"Mrs. Eliason?" Steve said.

"Oh, Detectives! You startled me!" Betty said.

"I'm so sorry." Steve said. "Do you have a few minutes? "We have a few questions to ask you."

"Sure." Betty said hesitantly. "What can I do for you?"

"Could we come in for just a bit?" Steve asked?

"Of course." Betty responded. "Let me just turn the hose off." She led the way to the front door.

"Come on in. Would you like something to drink?" Betty asked.

"No, thanks." Steve said. We just have a few questions to ask you about your former son-in-law."

"You mean Max?"

"Yes, Max." Steve answered. "We were hoping that you could give us some information about him, about his marriage to Meghan and maybe what's been going on with him since the divorce."

"Please, have a seat." Betty said, pointing to the chairs at the kitchen table. "What kind of trouble is he in now?"

"Oh, so he's been in trouble before." Steve said.

"Yes, he's been in trouble all right, marital trouble. I told Meghan when she first married him that he was no good. I knew he was cheating on her. A mother knows these things!" Betty said.

"Do you know who he cheated with?" Carl asked.

"Who knows!" Betty said. "It might as well have been a few the way he hurt my daughter. They used to live in the apartments on Pine Hill, just down the road. I think he still lives there if I'm not mistaken. Meghan left him there when she moved in with me when they divorced. He works with 'drywall', has his own company from what I've heard."

"Have you seen him lately?" Carl asked.

"No, I haven't, not since he helped remodel the house where the students live a couple of houses down. But that was a long time ago. Meghan told me he was working there." Betty answered.

"Anything else you'd like to tell us?" Carl asked.

"Well, he has a terrible temper." Betty said. "I was always afraid that he had hurt Meghan physically, but she said no."

"What time does Meghan usually get home from work?" Carl asked.

"She's usually home about 5:30pm. You're welcome to wait if you'd like." Betty said.

"Thanks, but I think we have all the information we need for now. If we need to talk to her, we know where to find her." Steve said, smiling.

Back in the car once again, Carl told Steve that he had an idea.

"Why don't we stop by Douglas' apartment on the way out of the neighborhood."

"Good idea!" Steve answered as he turned out of Alabaster Court and down to Pine Hill Road. The two Detectives walked down the walkway again and Steve knocked on the door to Apartment #9.

"Who is it?" A loud voice yelled out.

"Homicide Cold Case." Steve yelled back. "Looking for Max Douglas."

There were a few moments of quiet, finally the man on the other side of the door opened it to stretch the chain lock enough for him to see out and for Steve to look in.

"Max Douglas?" Steve asked.

"Yeah." The man said quietly.

"I'm Detective Steve Martinez and this is my partner, Detective Carl Spenser. Can we come in, please?"

Max closed the door, unhooked the chain lock and opened the door wide enough for the two Detectives to enter the apartment.

"What's all of this about?" He asked.

"We've re-opened a Homicide Cold Case from 2003, the murder of Charlotte Davis." Steve said bluntly. "We'd like to ask you a few questions about that case."

"Why would you want to talk to me? I don't know anything about it."

"You were married to Meghan Eliason, right?" Carl asked.

"Well, yeah, but what's that got to do with Charlotte Davis?" Max asked.

"Why don't you talk to Meghan?"

"We already have, now we need to talk to you…if you don't mind." Steve said.

Max scratched his head and offered Steve and Carl a seat in the living room. "Now what can I do for you?" He asked, sitting down in a kitchen chair.

"You were working for a construction crew in 2003, Coleman and Parkinson Company. Is that right?" Steve asked.

"Yeah, so what?" Max returned the question with a question.

"So…you must have become pretty familiar with the residents in the Court. The official documents from the construction company state that your crew was there for more than six months; that's a pretty long time to be in the same area with your ex without getting to know something about the people around you." Steve said. "You should have heard something about the murder, it's literally the talk of the Court."

Max became quiet and squirmed in the chair.

"I heard about it. She drowned, didn't she? In the pool in back of her parents' house?"

"That's right." Steve answered. "But she had been choked and hit in the head with some kind of instrument, and then she was pushed into the pool."

"So why are you telling me this?" Max answered.

"Because you may know more than you think you do. We'll have this conversation and perhaps you'll remember even more." Steve answered. Max squirmed in the chair again.

"I don't know anything; I'm just telling you what I heard." Max retorted.

"Your ex-wife, Meghan, was quite friendly with Charlotte Davis, wasn't she?" Steve asked.

"Why are you asking me these questions? I told you, all I know is what I've heard, and I only saw her when she was with her boyfriend in the Court. They were very open with their affection in the middle of the street."

"Did that make you angry?" Steve asked.

"Now why would that make me angry? She had a big mouth!" Max said, beginning to raise his voice.

"Who had a big mouth? Charlotte?"

"I'm not talking to you anymore!" Max shouted.

"Perhaps we need to take this conversation downtown to the Department." Steve said.

"Why? Do I need a Lawyer?"

"Now why would you need a Lawyer, Max?" Steve asked."

"I think you're trying to get me to admit to something I didn't do! You're trying to get me to admit that I killed that girl…"

"Did you?" Steve asked firmly.

"No, I didn't kill her!" Max shouted. "She drowned!"

The room fell silent for what felt like hours before Steve finally spoke.

"Could I use your restroom, man?" Steve asked. Max pointed to the bathroom. Once Steve was out of the room, Carl stood up and walked over to where Max was sitting in the kitchen.

"If you know something about this case, it's time for you to speak up. Seventeen years is a long time to keep something like this pinned up inside." Carl said quietly.

"I told you," Max said settling down, staring at Carl. "I didn't kill her…she drowned!"

"But you assaulted her and left her in the pool, didn't you? That's the difference between first degree murder and manslaughter. You choked her and hit her in the head with something…maybe a hammer? You certainly had access to a slew of construction tools that you could have used to knock her out."

Max was sweating as he looked up at Carl, his eyes swelling with tears.

"You've kept this secret for a long time. Time to put it to rest, for your sake and the sake of her family who still look for answers to their daughter's death." Carl said, putting his hand on Max's shoulder. "She had a big mouth, you said it yourself. What was she saying, Max?"

After another long pause, Max began to tell Carl what happened that night.

"She kept pestering me; telling me she was going to tell Meghan that I was with another woman. She knew I was trying to get Meghan back but she kept on threatening to tell Meghan. I couldn't let her do that!"

"So, you killed her." Carl said quietly.

"No." Max said. "She drowned."

"But you choked her, and you beat her in the head and you pushed her in the pool." Steve said, coming out of the bathroom. "Tell us what happened."

Max grabbed his head and began to weep.

"She was outside that night, feeding the neighborhood cat. It was dark and I had just finished some work I had been doing on the house. She walked over to me and started nagging me about Meghan. She said she had seen me with another woman, in the house we were remodeling."

"Were you with another woman in the house in the Court?" Steve asked.

"Yes." Max said, hesitantly. "I'm not proud of what I did but even so, I loved Meghan. I asked Charlotte what she wanted from me. She said she wanted me to leave Meghan alone. She had been threatening me that she was going to tell Meghan that I had been cheating. I kept telling her to leave me alone but she just kept on talking and talking! I grabbed her by the neck and I choked her, I just wanted her to shut up! She kicked me in the groin and started to run away, I picked up a hammer and followed her to the back yard of her parents' house. I hit her in the head with the hammer and she fell in the pool."

"Tell me about the red shoe, Max." Steve said.

"She walked out of the shoe on the way to her parents' house. I picked it up as I was running back to the house we were remodeling. I buried it in the front yard."

"Max Douglas…" Steve said as he put the handcuffs on Max. "You are under arrest for the murder of Charlotte Davis. You have the right to remain silent, anything you say can and will be held against you in a court of law. You have the right to an attorney; if you cannot afford one, one will be provided for you."

Two weeks later, Steve gave Carl a call to let him know that Max Douglas had been charged with Manslaughter, Assault and several other charges that would most probably find him imprisoned for a very long time.

"I also wanted to thank you for your help throughout this ordeal, brother." Steve said.

"No problem!" Carl answered. "I was particularly intrigued with your 'good cop, bad cop' routine when we were questioning Max Douglas."

"Yep, you picked up on that really fast!" Steve said. "You should consider transferring over to Homicide Cold Case. We make a pretty good team."

"I agree." Carl said. "But I like living in the present better than in the past!"

"I hear ya'…stay in touch!"

"You, too, brother. You, too."

BOOK VIII

The Residents of Alabaster Court

Final Chapter

"It's a beautiful day, mom." Meghan said as she looked out of the front door. "Come sit outside with me."

Betty walked to the front door and opened it.

"It is a beautiful day." She said, sitting down on a chair on the front porch.

"I remember sitting out here with your dad during the summer before he died. We didn't have to talk much, just sit together. I miss that quiet togetherness."

"I know you do, mom." Meghan said, putting her hand on her mother's knee. "There's not a day that goes by that I don't think about him."

"Me, too, honey." Betty said. "Me, too."

"Oh, look!" Meghan said excitedly, pointing across the Court to the Blackwell's house. "Amy's putting the pool out for the girls. Hi Amy." She yelled.

"Hello!" Amy yelled back. "Enjoying the day?"

"Yes." Amy answered. "Such a beautiful day!"

Peter walked out of the house with supplies to wash his truck. He waved at Betty and Meghan.

The solitude of the moment was interrupted by Detective Carl Spenser turning his car into the Court. He drove directly into Cora Jackson's driveway. Cora could be seen standing in the doorway, as if she had been waiting for him.

"I knew there was something going on between the two of them!" Carol Kavanaugh said to her husband as she leaned over to wave at Carl and Cora.

"Hello, Mrs. Kavanaugh." Cora said, waving back at her, acknowledging that she had seen Carol staring at her and Carl. "Beautiful day, isn't it?"

"Why, yes, it is!" Carol answered. "I'll bring some cucumbers and tomatoes over later. The garden is producing a lot this year."

"Oh, thank you. That would be so nice." Cora said as she and Carl walked into the house.

A few minutes later, Alex McKenzie was seen coming outside of his parents' house with a basketball. He began to bounce the ball around for a while and was soon joined by a couple of the students from the rental house.

"Alex, are you hungry?" Lori McKenzie yelled out from the window in the kitchen. "I can make a sandwich for you until dinner is done."

"Nah, maw." He answered. "I can wait."

The basketball game continued as Meghan went next door to JoAnna's and Melissa's house.

"What are you two doing in the house on such a beautiful day?" Meghan asked when JoAnna answered the door. "Let's have a picnic in the Court. We can invite everyone to join us and to bring a dish. I can always order some chicken and everyone else can bring sides, desserts, whatever. What do you think?"

"Where are we going to have this picnic?" Melissa asked.

"Right here, in the middle of the Court." Meghan said. She walked over to the Blackwell's house and asked Amy what she thought of the idea.

"I think it's a great idea!" Amy responded. "What about asking everyone to bring a chair and a card table or patio table to put the food on?"

"Great idea!" Meghan said. "I'll walk around the Court and let everyone know what we're doing."

"Mom!" Meghan yelled across the Court. "We're gonna' have a picnic!"

"A picnic?" Betty replied. "Where?"

"In the middle of the Court. It'll be fun!" Meghan said as she walked back across the court to her house. "I'll go get a few buckets of chicken and we can ask everyone else to bring sides. But first, I'm going to invite everyone to meet us in the court with their chair and a table."

Back at JoAnna's and Melissa's, Meghan explained the plan and told them to bring a side dish.

"Melissa makes the best vegetable Lasagna!" JoAnna said. "Right, Mel?"

"Sure." Melissa answered. "It'll only take about forty-five minutes to prepare."

"Excellent!" A very excited Meghan said as she ran toward the house where the students lived.

"Hey, guys." She said when one of the students opened the door. "We're having a picnic this evening, right in the middle of the Court. Bring a chair, table and a side dish. You do cook, don't you?"

"Phil!" The young men yelled out at the same time. "Phil is our cook, and he can really cook!"

"What are you cooking?" Meghan asked when the young man named Phil came out of the kitchen.

"Well, I was planning on baked spaghetti for tonight…" he said.

"That'll work." Meghan said. "Melissa next door is cooking vegetable lasagna. Maybe we'll just have a picnic with Italian foods!"

Meghan ran to the McKenzie's house and gave them instructions for the picnic.

"What a novel idea!" DJ said as he called out to Lori.

"Ooh!" Lori said with a smile. How about macaroni and cheese?" She asked. I was already cooking a roast with roasted potatoes…and macaroni and cheese! Just about ready."

Cora Jackson and Carl Spenser were standing on the front porch watching Meghan as she went from house to house announcing the first ever Alabaster Court picnic.

"Will you and Marie…and you, too, Detective Spenser come to the picnic?"

Cora and Carl looked at each other and nodded their heads 'yes'.

"What would you like me to bring?" Cora asked.

"Your Texas Toast, of course!" Meghan said. "And you can always throw in that delicious 'dirty rice'!"

Meghan knocked on the door to the Kavanaugh's house and Carol answered. "Hi, honey." Carol said. "What can I do for you?"

"I'm inviting everyone to a picnic this afternoon." Meghan replied. "Bring a chair, a small table and a side dish."

"Oh." Carol said. "And where will this picnic be held?"

"Right in the middle of the Court." Meghan answered. "Everyone's coming."

"Then we should, too." Carol answered. "We can bring a salad and other veggies from our garden. Oh, and a big jug of lemonade! Mark makes fabulous lemonade."

"That sounds perfect!" Meghan said. "See you in a couple of hours."

Back at the Blackwell's house, Meghan sat with Amy for a few minutes while the girls played in the swimming pool.

"The girls and I were going to bake cupcakes today. We'll bring dessert. What do you say about that, Meghan?"

"I say that's just great." Meghan answered. "I'm going to get the chicken and some mashed potatoes and gravy. See you in a little while."

Meghan made her way to JoElla's Catering and picked up three large trays of chicken and three large containers of mashed potatoes and gravy and drove back to her house. Betty was still sitting on the porch as Meghan brought the chicken into the house. The Court was very quiet. Meghan was sure everyone was getting their dishes together.

The first family seen coming out of their house with their dish was JoAnna and Melissa. JoAnna was carrying the card table that she and Melissa used to put their jigsaw puzzles together. Melissa had a large dish of vegetable lasagna. JoAnna ran back in the house to get the two chairs from their patio.

Meghan brought out a small table and two chairs for her and Betty. Betty followed close behind, making several trips in and out of the house to bring the chicken and mashed potatoes and gravy.

Peter could be seen next bringing out a table from the Blackwell's house followed by his two older daughters. A few minutes later, he could be seen bringing out the cupcakes, covered with fluffy icing and decorations. Amy met her family a few minutes later with the baby on her hip.

Carl Spenser carried a small table from the Jackson house with Marie close behind carrying a large tray of Texas Toast. Cora could be seen walking slowly with her father, Chester Dupuis, to a chair that Carl had placed next to the table. Marie went back into the house and reappeared with a large pot of 'dirty rice'

The students began to come out of their house, one by one, each carrying either the table, a chair or a cooler filled with cold beer. Phil was the last to come out with his baked spaghetti.

Mark and Carol Kavanaugh strategically placed their table in the center of the Court in front of their house. After bringing out the two chairs, Mark brought out the lemonade and Carol brought out a large salad bowl filled with vegetables from their garden.

Last, but certainly not least, the McKenzie family could be seen bringing out their table, chairs, macaroni and cheese and the family. Katie had driven up prior to the start of the picnic and was excited to see such a celebration going on while Alex was already there playing basketball.

Peter Blackwell used his truck speakers to filter music into the Court. He was soon joined by the students who had their own idea as to what music should be played!

As everyone began to be seated, Mark Kavanaugh cleared his throat and asked everyone if he could offer a short Prayer before everyone began to eat. It was agreed upon that a Prayer would clearly be appreciated. Everyone bowed their head.

"Heavenly Father…we thank you for this beautiful day and the idea to bring us together. Bless us all as we face our daily trials, knowing that we have you, and each other to depend upon. Bless this gathering, the food and future gatherings such as this. We thank you for these things and ask them in His Name…Amen."

The picnic lasted for several hours, in the middle of Alabaster Court. At one point, Carol Kavanaugh, who had been 'too busy' to attend their wedding, walked over to JoAnna and Melissa with a plate of vegetables.

"I thought you might like some of these veggies to take home with you. They come from our garden." She said, setting the plate on their table.

"Oh…" Melissa said. "That's very nice of you. Isn't that nice, JoAnna?"

"Yes…very nice. And thank you." JoAnna said, not sure what to think of the sudden hospitality.

Carol smiled and walked back over to her table with Mark.

A car was seen turning into the Court and parking in front of the Blackwell's house. It was a familiar car, one that had been in the Court many times with Carl Spenser. It was Steve Martinez.

"Glad you could come!" Carl said, extending his hand to shake Steve's. Carl went inside the Jackson house to get another chair for him as Steve went from table to table, shaking hands with all of the residents.

"Have a seat." Carl said.

"Thanks brother." Steve said, sitting down. "So, what's the 911?" Steve asked.

"Well." Cora said, lifting her left hand for everyone to see her new engagement ring. "We just got engaged!" Everyone clapped their hands with approval. There were hugs and well-wishes from all.

"But that's not all." Carl chimed in. "We're buying the house from the Davises. Since the case was solved, Mr. Davis asked us if we would like to buy the house. Of course, we said yes!"

"Since we're sharing good news…" JoAnna said, holding Melissa's hand. "We're adopting a baby! She should be born within the next six-months!"

Everyone began to clap their hands and cheered again.

"She?" Meghan asked.

"Yep." Melissa answered. "A baby girl. We couldn't be happier!"

"The Court was filled with 'oohs' and 'ahs' as the residents celebrated the good news.

"It's about time we have something to celebrate." Meghan said. "There's been far too many loses. Here's to much more good news!" She lifted her glass high as the other residents agreed and lifted their glasses.

The first-ever Alabaster Court picnic was a huge success. As it was beginning to get dark, there were more toasts to friendships and promises to have more gatherings and at least one picnic each year.

"By the way." Steve said to Carl as he walked him to his car. "Got another cold case that I've taken in interest in. Thought you might want to play cops and robbers once again. I know you said you like looking for the living rather than my kind of cases, but think about it."

"Who knows!" Carl said. "Let's talk about it this coming week sometime."

"At least you didn't say no!" Steve smiled and drove out of Alabaster Court.